"What is it that you want?"

"I want a sample, a bit of instruction," he said. There was a guileless look on his face, as if he was the perfectly innocent victim of all the world's harsh ways.

'A bit of instruction?" Abby asked. "What in the world are you talking about?"

"Well, I know the first part," he said. "I suppose you know the last. It goes like this." Both arms tightened around her, holding her helplessly against him. One of his hands came free and a finger went under her chin, tilting it upward. Selby bent further and touched her lips with his, just a gentle touch.

"Tender loving care," he said, almost in a whisper.

Emma Goldrick describes herself as a grandmother first and an author second. She was born and raised in Puerto Rico, where she met her husband, a career military man from Massachusetts. His postings took them all over the world, which often led to mishaps—such as the Christmas they arrived in Germany before their furniture. Emma uses the places she's been as backgrounds for her books.

Books by Emma Goldrick

EMMA GOLDRICK

The Unmarried Bride

Harlequin Books

TORONTO • NEW YORK • LONDON
AMSTERDAM • PARIS • SYDNEY • HAMBURG
STOCKHOLM • ATHENS • TOKYO • MILAN
MADRID • WARSAW • BUDAPEST • AUCKLAND

ISBN 0-373-11681-0

THE UNMARRIED BRIDE

CHAPTER ONE

ABIGAIL CONSTANCE SPENCER arched her back to relieve the strain, swept up her skirts under her, and sat down on the stone step that guarded the front porch. Behind her, through the open door, the hall gleamed and the kitchen sparkled. This morning at six Abby had looked pert and determined, while the house had looked as if Attila the Hun had dropped by; now, in the softness of a late summer twilight, the house sparkled and gleamed, while Abby drooped.

She dropped her head forward onto her arms, her straw blond hair falling like a mist around her head. It had all been worth it, she told herself. Uncle Theodore, after eighty-nine cantankerous years, had upped and died, leaving the tiny island and his good wishes to his great-grandniece Abigail Spencer.

"My house and anything she can find in it," his will said. "She is the only relative I have who refuses to bicker with me." It must have been sarcasm, she chuckled to herself. Of all his living relatives, Abby was the one Uncle Teddy had spent years carefully avoiding, which made the bang-up arguments he was always seeking with other family members impossible with her. And besides, she liked the old codger.

Certainly he would never have considered it an advantage that his house stood isolated at the top of one of the two small hills on Umatec Island, looking down on to the hurrying waters of Narraganset Bay and the Atlantic Ocean. Isolated, but picture-perfect for a woman who made a precarious living reviewing the endless horde of mediocre novels that rolled off the presses, all for the edification of the readers of the *Washington Sunday Mirror*.

She had come late in the holiday season because of Aunt Letty. Great-Aunt Letty, that was. "You're worn to a frazzle, girl. Practically all bones, you are. You suffer from overmanagement," her great-aunt had lectured. "Your mother, your brothers, that crazy newspaper editor—all of them sworn to manage your life for you. Go up to Umatec, and relax."

So here I am, Abby told herself. Bound and determined to relax. Just as soon as I get all those little jobs finished, I'm determined to relax!

Soft fur caressed Abby's ankle. She opened one green eye. Cleo, her almost purebred collie, was rubbing the silver gray fur on top of her head against Abby's bare feet. "Purebred," Abby said, teasing. "Hah! Your father was a sheepdog and your mother came from the South Sea Islands—or something." Her dog stared at her from solid green eyes, and turned disdainfully away.

Uncle Teddy had hated dogs! He had certainly been far out to sea concerning Cleo, she thought. Despite the complimentary thought the collie offered one very snobbish sneer down her long nose and wandered away. Tired, Abby dropped her head on her arms again and closed her eyes. How about that? she told herself. Even your own dog won't talk to you! And then she dozed.

"What are you doin' to my house?" An insistent male demand, coming just forward of her chin. Abigail snapped her head up and opened one eye. Umatec was one tiny spot of an island, one of the chain of Elizabeth Islands that stretched from the underflank of Cape Cod down into Long Island Sound. Certainly it was no place to expect a determined four-foot taffy-headed male dressed in a nondescript pair of swimming trunks and a belligerent look. The look covered more than the swimming trunks did.

Abby had seen her share and more of belligerent males; it was one of the reasons she had fled the city with her bulging briefcase. Nothing seemed to sting the psyche of endless male detective story writers more than to read her usually gentle comments in the *Sunday Mirror*. Why her editors referred to her as the "vitriol lady" she could never understand. And if the writers ever discovered that Cicero was a female the skies would fall.

But this particular male, although out of place, did not seem large enough to cause any serious trouble. She bit on the challenge. "As it happens, it's *my* house, young man, and I'm cleaning it. Just what the devil are *you* doing here?"

The freckled face screwed itself up. "No, it ain't your house. I live here. Me and my dad." And then a wave of suspicion. "Did my dad sell you my house?"

"I don't suppose he did." Abby patted the step beside her in a tacit offer of debate. The little boy looked her up and down cautiously and backed off one step. He folded his hands behind his back, as if he was not willing to take any chances with the woman in front of him.

"I inherited this house—and the island too, for that matter, from my uncle Theodore," Abby continued. "And now that I've got the house cleaned up I intend to live here."

The boy's upper lip began to quiver. "You can't do that to my house," he said. "I'm gonna tell my dad. He'll have you arrested and thrown in jail. What do you think about that?"

"I can't say that I'm terribly pleased. Where is this dad of yours? Hiding?"

"My dad is the *strongestest* man in the world. He wouldn't hide from no girl."

Abby stood up slowly. His eyes traced her movement. Without heels Abigail was just slightly over five feet ten. In her favorite two-inchers she could look down on many a six-footer. The boy was impressed. He backed off a step or two. "An' he's awful brave, too. He wouldn't be scared by no girl. Not even no *big* girl," he amended.

"Well, I'm sure he wouldn't," Abby assured the boy. What do you suppose? she asked herself. Eight years old? Hard to tell. Abby was the only female in an extended family, all of whose members thought it proper for females—meaning Abigail—to fetch and carry, mind their manners and be otherwise unobtrusive. So she had *some* perspective on the dominant male. And consider. He *thinks* his big old dad might have sold *his* house out from under him. How about *that* for confidence?

"I'm thirsty and tired and dirty, and I need a bath—in *my* bathtub, young man. Why don't you run along to wherever this daddy of yours is located?"

"Boy, you're gonna be sorry." The boy backed off another couple of paces, almost tripping over Cleo, who had been attracted by the voices. The dog was no tiny thing. In fact, Cleo could weigh in as a junior weight wolf, but hadn't the energy to be mean. The boy, not understanding all this, saw only Cleo's outside frame and sharp teeth, not the tender soul within. He gulped, glared at the pair of them, then abandoned the field. As he disappeared over the top of the hill Abby could faintly hear him yell, "You're gonna be sorry! You just wait!"

Her dog gave her a quizzical look—the sort that might be interpreted as, Well, what have you done now, Abigail Spencer?

"If I knew I'd tell you. It's all fairly confusing as there isn't enough room on this island for a mouse to hide away all day. He seemed to be talking as if there was some permanence to his visit. Oh, well." Abby shook her head and headed back into the house. "I'm going to have a bath. And I might take a look in the other bedrooms to see if anything is happening. Care to join me?"

Cleo understood words like "bath" and "dinner," even though the need for a bath was totally beyond comprehension. But she was a willing companion, no matter what the object. The pair of them strolled into the house and up the stairs. As they went into the hall Cleo found her little yellow ball, her favorite toy, and picked it up.

At the top landing Abby stopped and contemplated. It was a huge house, with rooms to spare, all built as additions on the original saltbox. Most of the floors of the additions did not quite match the original construction. As a result there were steps up or down, or slanted floors galore at the junction points. But the upstairs hall, part of the original construction, looked to be smooth and level and about the size of two lanes at a bowling alley.

Uncle Teddy had been as eccentric as his house. In the course of a wild and woolly life he had won and lost four fortunes, and on the day he died, fighting all the way, he had been drawing up a scheme to make another. His house was built for a monarch, but Uncle had hardly occupied it for more than a summer month each year. And, with the flavor of the turn of the century, it was referred to as a summer cottage.

Abby stroked Cleo's neck. "And he would have made another fortune too, if time hadn't run out on him." The dog woofed agreement. They walked to the end of the hall and looked in the rooms along the way. Abby hadn't cleaned any of the other bedrooms other than the one she normally used when she came to Umatec Island. Her assigned room was the one farthest from the bathroom, but she had always enjoyed the walk down

the hallway. She found luggage and signs of inhabi-
tation in two of the other rooms. Someone was evidently
living, very neatly, in Uncle Theodore's old room and
someone else was living, fairly messily, in the room next
to hers. Interesting.

The bathroom took up the entire east end of the house.
The tub was big enough for three or four and made of
Vermont marble. It stood on a two-foot platform above
the tiled floor. The entire east wall was glass. The old
man had liked to soak in his tub with a drink in one
hand and a cigar in the other, and watch the boats go
up the channel.

"Dancing girls," Abby said, chuckling. "Oriental
music. Houris?" Her dog, who had followed close
behind her, backed off into the corner next to the door.
"Some day," she mused, "I'm going to find out just
what a houri is." She had a vague idea from reading
translations of *The Thousand and One Nights*, but could
never drive herself to actually look up the word, afraid
the dictionary might tell her more than she cared to
know.

Abby turned on the hot-water tap. From a distance
she could hear a click and a roar as the generator came
on line. In a moment the hot water poured out of the
ornate spout very satisfactorily.

"I'll say one thing for Uncle Teddy," she told her dog.
"He never stinted on something he really wanted." Cleo
laid her head on the cold floor between her front paws.
Abby swayed to what she thought was oriental music,
and slowly stripped as she gyrated and sang. It was more
Hawaiian than oriental, but for a girl who hardly ever
stirred more than twenty-five miles from Washington it
was a good approximation. A hot bath was the Spencer
family recipe for relaxation from cares and Abby was
falling into the family habit and forgetting the unex-

plained people on the island. They could wait—the bath, however, was a necessity!

With a copious gesture she sprinkled bath powder over the water. There were three different kinds. She used some of each. Suds swelled up and over the sides of the tub as she climbed in, sat down, and sighed with relief. The suds came up past her chin. She shoveled a path for herself, and then leaned back and closed her eyes.

The warmth welcomed her, soothing her body and her mind. Gradually her hands drifted smoothly down her long, soft curves. She sighed again, and blew away a suds cloud that threatened her nose. "There's no doubt about it," she told Cleo. "I'm in love with Harry Farnsworth." And again she sighed at her foolishness. Harry Farnsworth was a character in one of Selby Jones's detective stories. A fictional character. Tall, blond and powerful, with a saber scar high on his right cheek. How stupid can a girl get, to fall in love with a fictional character? Disgusted with herself, she pushed it all out of her mind, and began scrubbing.

The sound of a door slamming brought her up sharply. Umatec was too small an island for more than one house. The only thing that came to mind was the small boy and the owners of the luggage in the bedrooms. Access to the island is by small boat only and I know I didn't invite anyone, she thought. So why should I lock the doors? The little boy—where the devil did *he* come from? And this father he was bragging about? An escaped criminal from the maximum security prison?

Footsteps. They rattled up the bare wooden stairs and then disappeared into the depths of the hall carpet. Oh, God! Abby sank down into the suds, wishing for a periscope or a weapon—or both. Her hands slid around the sides of the tub. Nothing.

"So. That's where you're hiding." An indignant accusation leveled by an angry little boy.

"I am *not* hiding, I'm bathing. What the devil are you doing in my bathroom? And what, may I ask, is your name?"

"My name is Harry. My father is coming. You'd better get out of there. If he finds you there—Lordy, if he finds *me* here!"

Abby sat up and pushed the suds away from her face. The little fellow was trembling. Scared, or just cold? He was barefoot, and still wore nothing but the tatty bathing suit.

"Your father won't hurt you," she said. "That's against the law."

"Law? My father doesn't care about no laws. And you don't know him. He'll murder me when he catches me."

"I find that hard to believe," Abby said. "After all, we live in a civilized community."

"Yeah, civilized. I used some of his good paper to draw on yesterday and he's just found out. He'll kill me, lady. Believe! Where can I hide?"

"He wouldn't dare——" Abby stopped in midsentence. *Somebody* dared. The downstairs door slammed again. Really slammed, so that parts of the old house shook.

"Harry? Harry!" There were noises as the man downstairs stomped through the living room, the kitchen, the study, and back to the foot of the stairs.

"Harry Farnsworth, you'd better get down here before I tan your hide. Harry!"

Harry Farnsworth? It couldn't be, but there it was. I'm dreaming, Abby told herself. Dreaming it all! Harry Farnsworth is a fictional character in a book!

But the boy believed that Harry was reality. He listened for a moment as the footsteps came up the stairs—heavy footsteps, something on the order of King Kong. The boy looked around for a place to hide. The footsteps reached the upper landing. The next scene was choreographed out of an old Bixby movie. The boy looked over his shoulder at the sudsy tub, then back toward the stairs. Abby, on cue, not willing to share her tub, came up out of the water covered from head to toe with suds, slipped on the marble floor, and skidded off into a corner. She clutched madly as she skidded, and came to a halt with two massive bathtowels wrapped around her.

The boy screwed up his courage and jumped headfirst into the tub, instantly disappearing into the blanket of suds.

"Well, I thought the boy was lying," drawled a deep male voice, supported by a massive pair of shoulders and as stern a look as Abby had seen since she left St. Alban's Catholic high school. The good Mother Superior, somewhat puzzled by the gangling size of the girl, had spent years trying to convert her into a neat, obedient doll. With not much luck. And now this—whatever—and in her bathroom! She jerked herself up to a sitting position and brushed away enough suds to be able to see clearly.

"And just what the devil are you doing in my bathroom?" she demanded.

"Your bathroom."

"My bathroom. This isn't Highway Ninety-five. And I'm taking a bath."

"Your bathroom?"

"We said that once. Is there something wrong with your hearing?"

"That's possible," he said.

Such a nice voice, Abby told herself. If I weren't so angry with him I'd—well, I won't! Good-size, too. Well proportioned. Nice tan. An outdoor man. So maybe we could talk this out?

"My bathroom," she said. "My uncle left it to me. I mean not just the bathroom, but the house and the island and—well, everything. And now if you would kindly remove yourself I'll get dressed and—what are you doing?"

"You claim you're taking a bath, but you're sitting in the corner," he said menacingly. "So why is there another hand in the tub? And if the other half of this act is my son Harry there'll be hell to pay." He came up on to the pedestal step and bent over the tub.

"No," Abby protested. "Don't——"

Cleo had been following the play of the game, and thought she understood the rules. She came up to her feet, walked over behind the man and barked. A very impressive bark, Cleo's, one that might have come from any self-respecting monster. The man hesitated.

"Does he bite?"

"All the time. She bites all the time."

"Harry. Come out of there!" No longer a gentle voice, but rather the kind that tamed hurricanes.

"Oh, no," Abby said. "She——"

Whatever nonsense Abby thought her dog would get into was hardly comparable to what actually happened. One more "woof" and Cleo reared back on her hind legs and gave the man a considerable bump on his posterior. It was not an excessively strong attack, but he was already half bent over the tub, and Cleo did the rest. He tottered for a moment, then went headfirst into the tub. A wave of water came over the edge and splashed down onto the tile floor, taking some of the suds with it. With a squeak of alarm Abby struggled to her feet, wrapped herself securely in the towels, and sidled toward the door.

"Gotcha," the male voice in the tub commented. The boy appeared, coming up out of the suds, suspended by his father's right arm. A second or two later the man appeared, spitting suds in all directions. He groped for the wet step and set the boy down on the floor. As soon as Harry's feet hit the floor he started running. But his father maintained a grip on his bathing suit. The lad was making running motions but getting nowhere. The man emerged. Another wave of water splattered out of the tub. Abby, too astonished to notice anything else, just stood there. That last splash of water had washed away almost all the suds on the floor. The man stared at her, while firmly holding the boy's head in the other direction. "Put something on!" he commanded.

Up to that moment Abby Spencer had been riding high on her anger. Now, with the man's remark, she looked hastily down. The towel covered her. Not artistically, perhaps, but covered. Her only hope was disdain. "As it happens, Whoever-you-are, I'm a good deal better covered than either one of you."

His father took a good long look, then pushed the boy toward the door. "Out, son."

That's all he can do, Abby thought. While I'm standing here shivering he's chasing the boy out of the room. "You could go yourself," she muttered at him. The towel was slipping off her left shoulder. His eyes bugged.

"Look, Mrs.——"

"Miss," Abby said. "Miss." And then very slowly, "Would you do me the favor of getting out of my bathroom?" It wasn't exactly a polite question. The bathsheet was soaking wet and clinging to her frame like a piece of wet tissue—very revealing and form-fitting.

She could see by the look on his face that the towel promised much more than she was even willing to think about. But if she *was* going to think about it he just about fitted her dream qualifications.

"Daddy?" The boy twisted around to see the goings on, and was immediately twisted back again by his father.

"I'm sorry, Miss——"

"Spencer," she yelled at him. "Now will you get out of here?"

"Out of here? Oh, yes." A big grin sparkled across his face, lighting him and half the world. He looked boyish—no longer threatening. He left the room, shepherding his son in front of him. Taking his own darned time about it too, Abby told herself.

He left the door open as he marched his son out in front of him. A chill raced up Abby's spine. She wrapped the bathsheet more securely around her. The chill was not entirely due to the wind blowing into the room, she assured herself. A large portion of it was due to the man himself. Not *a* man, but rather *this* man. He was having an effect on her that she wasn't sure she wanted. And yet——?

Not being the tidiest person in her family, Abby turned the switch that emptied the tub, and then looked around at the flood of water on the floor. For some reason it seemed to be eddying over into the corner. Closer inspection showed that a drain was built in that corner and the floor was slightly tilted. "Oh, Uncle Teddy," she giggled. "Just what were you up to in this magnificent tub?"

From downstairs there came the noise of harsh words. It seemed that little Harry was listening while his father did all the talking. Curiosity had always been one of Abby's major weaknesses. She hurried down the hall to her bedroom, drying herself while she went, and when she reached her room she snatched up a green floor-length beach robe. Cleo padded docilely along beside her.

No reason to dress, she told herself. He won't be around that long. She fastened the robe, made a vague effort to dry her hair, but gave it up in disgust. Curiosity and anger were driving her much faster than beauty. Together she and Cleo went down the stairs as fast as they could walk.

The men were making themselves at home in the living room. Or, as Abby called it, the blue room. It was a dark room with few windows and many drapes, all blue. It gave the appearance of a cave, a blue cave. Since there was no electric power available on the island except from the house generator, the room was softly lit by a pair of propane-powered lamps.

The two males had evidently run through their arguments. The elder was sitting in one of her overstuffed chairs. He was still soaking wet and he was toweling the boy, who stood between his legs with a big grin on his small face.

"There," the boy said. "There's four of us here in this room and only one of us is wearing shoes. Take your shoes off, Daddy."

"Four of us?"

"Yeah. You, me and her and her dog."

"Ah, I forgot the dog. But no, I can't do that," the man returned. "She—will be leaving any minute now, and she'll need my help. That's what men do for women—they help."

Abby walked over to the huge couch and sat down, pulling her feet up beneath her. She had walked down the stairs torn between curiosity and growing anger that *anyone* would be on her island and disturb her peace. "Now then, Mr.——?"

"Farnsworth," he answered the prompt. "Selby Farnsworth. And this is my son Harry——"

"My name is Henry," the child interrupted. "Henry Farnsworth."

A fine pair of liars, both of you, Abby thought. How could he have got the child so well-trained? Harry Farnsworth is a fictional character. Who should know better than me? Selby Jones had written three books and she had panned the first two while the third was—well, almost perfect.

"Farnsworth," she mused. "It seems to me that that's a name I'd choose if I was going to hide out. So tell me, Mr. Farnsworth——" and you could hear the question mark in the name "—how long have you been on the island? I've been cleaning the house all day and I've not seen hide nor hair of either of you. This is a very small island. I can't believe you've been on *my* island all day without coming up to the house."

"My son and I have been on the island for three weeks," the man retorted. "We went over to Hyannis to do some shopping and sight-seeing. I have a lease on this island and this house for six weeks, ending on September fifteenth."

"I don't see how that's possible," Abby said. "We've got three weeks until September fifteenth and I certainly haven't signed any lease with you. I don't intend to wait that long to be rid of you, either. You'd just better pack and leave. You can take the boat you came over in from Hyannis today and go back to the mainland. And while you're there maybe you should just sit down and check your so-called lease."

"I don't have a boat. We hired someone to drop us off here and I've hired him to come again in three weeks on the fifteenth to pick us up. I don't need to check the lease," he snapped. "It's all legal and aboveboard. I made sure of that before I signed it."

"My dad's a——"

"Harry, shut up!"

The boy clapped his hands over his mouth. "We ain't s'posed to tell," he added in a little whisper.

"I'm a lawyer. I've already checked the lease."

"I can see that you must have." Abby restrained a grin. It was fun to be talking to this—lawyer. "And who signed the lease?"

"Miss Spencer," he said, and then sat up and looked at her suspiciously. "Miss Abigail Spencer?"

"Did Miss Spencer sign it? A.L. Spencer?" He nodded. "Was she a little old lady? White hair, a little thin on top? Stands about five feet three? Looks like a chipper little bluebird?"

"Exactly. What are you trying to tell me?"

"Nothing particularly important," Abby said, teasing him along. "As it happens, I'm the only Abigail in the Spencer family. You're talking about my great-aunt Amaryllis Letitia. Too bad. Aunt Letty loves to play the horses. I suspect she and your money are already down in Florida, or wherever the ponies are running these days."

"Then you're the one that——"

"Inherited this place, lock, stock and barrel," Abby said. "My house, my island——"

"An' don't forget the treasure," the boy said. "There's a big treasure here, ain't there?"

"I haven't any idea if there is any treasure. My uncle used to say there was but he wasn't willing to let anyone come and dig for it. '*My* treasure,' Uncle Teddy used to say——" A dull sound in the background interrupted her; the windows rattled in their frames. "He was a peculiar fellow, my uncle. But he left this island to me."

Abby got up and went to the window. "Look, it's getting pretty late, and from the looks of things there's a storm brewing out there. Hadn't you two better start thinking of how to be on your way?"

"On our way hell," the man said. "You—at least your family—owes me three more weeks of living on this island, and I mean to have it."

"Sue me," Abby prompted.

"I will," he returned. "We're not leaving this island until our lease is up." A crash of thunder sounded from outside. Abby walked back to the window and pulled back the drapes. Low dark clouds were racing across the sky, bending the few island trees before them.

"Looks like a northeaster," Abby commented as she dropped the drapes. "I wouldn't put a dog out on a night like this. You can spend the night. Lord knows we have plenty of rooms. Tomorrow we'll talk it over like sensible adults, and see what we can see."

"My boat isn't coming back until September fifteenth," he reiterated. "We're staying at least that long."

"I can take you back to the mainland tomorrow. I have a little runabout. And don't shout at me. I don't happen to be a lawyer, but I do know my rights." She dropped on to the old-fashioned ottoman and regretted it immediately. The thing seemed to have been stuffed with horsehair.

The boy squirmed around, a cherub smile on his full-fleshed face. "That oughta be fun," he chortled. "Do you own that little white boat with the yellow stripe on it?"

"Why did you ask?" Abby pulled herself up to her feet. "What is it about that little white boat with the yellow stripe that makes you so happy?"

"Well, whoever left it in the cove didn't tie it up very well. When I seen it half an hour ago it was drifting out in the channel."

"Drifting?" Abby liked nothing better than a calm, peaceful life. Boats didn't drift, not when they were the only means of getting off Umatec Island. Strange men didn't appear out of the storm and declare themselves to be fictional characters. Women like me—all twenty-nine years of me—don't find themselves marooned on a deserted island with a little boy and a pirate, she told herself.

Harry's father looked down at him with a very suspicious look in his eyes. "The boat just drifted away?"

"Well, it certainly got loose. The rope came all apart and it just drifted away."

Abby looked at them both. "I tie my lines with good knots," she said. "The knot didn't come out by itself."

"Harry," his father said accusingly. The little boy blushed and stubbed his toe on the floor.

"Well, I just had to see what it was, you know. It had a engine and it was floating nice and I thought I could get in and maybe take a little ride. And——"

"And what?" his father asked in the tone used in a courtroom to ask the accused when he had stopped beating his wife.

Abby winced in sympathy. There seemed to be very little compassion in that voice and Harry looked as if he needed very large doses of compassion and love on a daily basis. Even an amateur like Abby could tell that this little boy was on an emotional seesaw. He smiled and laughed and then was so serious and so angry. He bounced emotionally and it was very erratic. She didn't think that Selby Farnsworth, no matter how good-looking, was the ideal person to deal with Harry's problems.

"The motor wouldn't start," the boy replied firmly. "I untied the knot and the darn motor wouldn't start. It's all your fault, lady. It's not fair, keepin' a boat when the motor don't start. There's laws against that!"

The anger which had sparked his father's face faded into a grin. "There probably is a law," he conceded. "Lord knows there seem to be more laws than people nowadays. So what did you do next?"

Zeus, Abby told herself. Sitting up there on Mount Olympus ready to cast a thunderbolt or two? Her eyes studied his face. Burned by the outdoor sun, smooth skin sporting a Roman nose, and a—dear God—a scar just under his left eye!

"I—uh—just climbed over the side and swam back to shore," the boy said. "It was all because of that darn motor. It wouldn't start. It ain't my fault."

"Oh, boy," his father said. "It's been a whole week of 'one of those days.'"

Abby looked at both of them and swallowed her tongue. Out of the corner of her eye she just happened to see the look on the elder Farnsworth's face. Glee? Anticipation? Satisfaction?

"Well, Miss Spencer," he said. "That just about wraps it up, doesn't it? None of us can leave without a boat. Your boat's probably down off Cutty Hunk by now, and ours won't be back for another three weeks or more. So, unless you've got some magic signal to summon help, I guess we're all stuck here together, right?"

"Now just a darn minute," Abigail Spencer said firmly. "Let's not get carried away here. I've agreed that you can stay overnight. After that, well——"

The grin vanished from his face, to be replaced by a predatory look. His teeth gleamed in the soft light of the room. He's looking for a place to bite, Abby told herself as she squirmed back in her chair, as far away from him as she could get.

"Let me explain something to you," he said. Abby ducked away from the voice of doom. All her relationships with lawyers had been uniform—uniformly bad.

"First of all," he continued, "if we don't get occupancy of this island until September fifteenth, I will certainly file a civil suit against your aunt Letty. For triple damages, of course." He used a finger to mark an illusionary figure one in the air.

"And then I think we might institute some criminal charges. Using the mails to defraud. Yes, that's a nice one. Ten years in the slammer, as I recall. And then there's the matter of embezzlement. Not to be overlooked, that. Probably another two years or so. And I'm sure I can think of a few more items, given a moment or two."

"You—you wouldn't——" Abby stammered hopefully. "She's a sweet little old lady, and——"

"And she'll be a lot older when she comes out," he added. "No doubt about it. I'll have her little posterior in a sling, lady, unless——"

"Unless?" Abby's voice broke into a squeak.

"Unless we get to stay here until September fifteenth."

Abby choked on her own hurried breath. "So stay," she half whispered. "So stay and be happy. Aunt Letty's too old for jail sentences!"

"How kind you are." That grin returned. "How about that, Harry? The lady wants us to stay."

"I don't know that she means it," the boy returned.

"She means it," his father assured him. "Or else! Now then, lady, we are all here together. Don't you think that as our hostess you should start making us dinner?" Mr. Farnsworth had put the persuasive tone into his voice, as if to try and make her feel that she would either be *obliged* to cook or she would *want* to cook for his son and himself.

Abby had never felt that cooking dinner was a gender-oriented task. "I'm not hungry tonight and you aren't really here at my invitation. So if you want to eat dinner the kitchen is down the hall."

"Harry and I have been surviving on peanut butter sandwiches and I'm sick of them," he said. "And you *did* invite us."

"Didn't you bring anything else to eat?" Abby forced herself to ask, trying hard not to offer any of the food she had brought over with her.

"We brought only canned goods and, since neither of us likes washing dishes, we eat peanut butter and jelly sandwiches."

"I like peanut butter and jelly sandwiches," Harry contributed to the conversation.

"Well, there you are. Enjoy your meal, gentlemen. I'll see you in the morning."

Before either of them could tell her anything more that she didn't want to hear, she scuttled out of the room and back up the stairs. Cleo paced along behind her. The dog was older than anyone cared to think, and running upstairs was difficult. As Abby ran she could hear the sound of their male laughter, and no amount of holding her hands over her ears could shut it out.

She almost tripped over her trailing robe, but managed to catch herself on the smooth oak banister. She thought for a moment that the man was surely going to blister the boy's bottom; instead the laughter rolled on. And I, she told herself bitterly, am the butt of it all. Well, we'll see about that.

Her door slammed behind her, almost amputating Cleo's tail. A very satisfactory slam. Just enough to relieve her tensions. Just barely enough. And how would your Sunday school class react to all of this? It was a thought somewhat stronger than she could bear. She walked over to the bed and fell across it, peering toward the half-open window. The boy she could understand. She had ten of them just like him in her Sunday school class. But the father?

He was more than she could handle, even on her best day, this Selby Farnsworth. He wasn't handsome, not on your life. Too rugged. Too outdoorsy for a girl who spent most of her life among books. Too darn sure of himself. And a lawyer to boot? Lord protect us! she thought. But maybe—only a couple of weeks? Just long enough to teach him a lesson? Hit him in his ego, the way I handle my brothers. That ought to do the trick!

A lawyer, she mused; that ranked him just below used-car salesmen and just above politicians on her personal list. She giggled at the idea. The curtains swayed in the wind, and a thin spray of water reached as far as the bed.

"Oh, hell," she muttered, and dashed to close the window. *Oh, hell?* "Yes," she said firmly as she eased the window down. "Oh, hell! A girl is entitled to at least one swear word now and then. Especially in the privacy of her own room." Cleo, who had been lying down in the corner listening, made a funny noise, almost like laughter.

There were a few of her things piled at Abby's feet. She looked down. A suitcase, a bag of fruit, and a—— She gulped. It was decision time already. "So, unless you've got some magical signal to summon help, I guess we're all stuck here together, right?" he had said, and then that funny laugh and that leer.

"Well, we *can* call for help," she said, giggling. "But you'll never know, Mr. Know-it-all Farnsworth. Not until I'm ready to tell you." With a very large grin on her face she picked up the leather case containing her portable cellular telephone and her big battery-operated AM-FM radio. She made sure they were both turned off, then stored them on the upper shelf of her wardrobe.

With this happy thought she took a piece of fruit from the bag and one of the manuscripts she had to read with her to bed. She would just read a while and then she'd have to go and wash her hands. The orange was a particularly juicy one.

"Yes, Mr. Selby Farnsworth, now we play the game *my* way," she murmured.

CHAPTER TWO

ON THE way back from the bathroom that evening, Abby passed by Selby's door and heard a familiar "tap, tap, tap." There was a light under the door and inside a typewriter was being used. She knew the sound well.

"Selby Farnsworth. If you aren't Selby Jones, the author of my favorite hero, I'll be darned," she whispered. "You've come all the way up here to write a book. There's no doubt about it. Is there no limit to your cleverness? You're a lawyer and a writer, perhaps something else as well? I wonder what?"

Quietly, so as not to give the whole show away, she stole back to her own room and walked in, closing the door behind her. Cleo was already coiled up on the throw rug by the bed. Abby had to climb over the dog to get into the bed and once she was in she knew she would have difficulty getting to sleep. It was too early for her to go to bed! Besides, there were too many secrets to be analyzed. Nevertheless, in the middle of her argument, sleep came quietly over her and in just a few seconds she was out.

It was the noise that woke her up. What was it? Someone was crying just outside her door. Someone who was trying to smother the noise. Cleo was awake as Abby pulled herself out of bed, awake and shuffling to the door to sniff at whatever might be outside. Ghosts? Abby asked herself. Of course not! That was one thing which Uncle Teddy would have never allowed in his house.

She unlocked her door and pulled it open. Little Harry Farnsworth was sitting on the top step of the stairs, nestled hard up against the newel post of the mahogany banister. He was crying, a soft, muted cry as if he wanted to ease his agony without letting the world know he was hurting.

After a moment's consideration, Abby padded over to the head of the stairs and sat down beside him. He stirred a little—just enough to give her sitting space. She put her arm around him. His head lifted away from the newel post and leaned on her. A soft, sweet head was resting on her breast, crying softly.

"What's the matter, Harry?" she murmured.

"I don't know," the boy said. "I was dreaming about—about—well, you wouldn't care about that. You don't have to sit with me. You could go back to bed. I'm all right." There was a large amount of pride in his voice, more than his age or size should have contained.

"I'm sure you are," Abby said. She applied a little pressure and pulled the boy against her until the whole length of him was resting against her body. The sobbing gave way to intermittent tears. "Do you want me to call your dad?"

"No!" said the boy sharply. "Not that! He'd be awful mad."

The crying had stopped completely. He rubbed his nose with one hand and poked at his eyes with the knuckles of the other, still leaning against her. She could feel the muscles in his body relax. Silence played across the room. Nothing but the sound of the storm could be heard.

As the wall clock struck the quarter hour he lifted his head out of the warm, soft nest between her breasts.

"You know, you're awful soft. My daddy is hard, like iron. I think my mommy used to be soft like you."

Wordlessly, Abby stroked his shoulder and brushed his hair out of his eyes. She maintained the pressure that kept him against her and waited. By the next striking of the quarter hour, he was asleep. His features were marked by tears but there was a little smile on his face.

"What do I do now?" Abby muttered.

She almost jumped out of her skin when a deep voice behind her said, "Now you pick him up and put him back in bed."

She turned around and looked over her shoulder. Selby Farnsworth, dressed in the bottom half of an old pair of pyjamas, was staring down at her, brooding over the pair of them. She looked back at him for a moment or two and then sighed. "I can't—he's too heavy for me."

He stepped down a stair or two to position himself in front of them and reached down gently to pick up his son. As his arm encircled the child the back of his wrists touched and then caressed her breasts. Abby took a deep audible breath as all her systems snapped to attention, and then he was gone.

She trailed after him into the boy's room. He put the child down gently, arranged the blankets over him, checked the window to make sure it was shut and then tiptoed out into the hall. Abby took a moment to lean over the bed and kiss Harry's forehead. He stirred uneasily, which made her back up hurriedly.

"Go'nite, Mommy," Harry murmured.

Abby moved quietly out into the hall, and in the darkness ran into Selby. His arms came around her, perhaps to steady her, or perhaps—oh, stop that, she told herself angrily, stop romanticizing.

"Does he always have nightmares like this?" she whispered.

"No," he said bitterly. "I almost had him over these dreams. Thanks for your help."

To be totally honest, it didn't sound as if he really meant any thanks at all. It was almost as if he was embarrassed to have his son be the center of such notice, Abby told herself. And he'd said dreams, not nightmares.

"I couldn't just leave him there, crying," she snapped, just barely remembering to keep her voice down. "Any woman would have gone to comfort him."

"That's what you think," he said disgustedly. "His mother wouldn't." And he marched smartly down the hall toward his own room.

As she stood watching him move away from her, her hands doubled into fists. "I could give you such a whack," she whispered. But the lessons on ladylike behavior which her mother had drilled into her as a child all came to mind and so, with only some mild swearing under her breath, she returned to her room.

Sleep, this time, did not come quietly, or gently. She finally fell asleep and wrestled with her own terrible dream, which lasted until morning. In that dream she was chasing Selby Farnsworth with a big stick and she finally caught him. But before she had the satisfaction of whacking him the dream came to a halt, and then went back to its beginning, like a recorded tape whose end had been spliced to its start to make a circle. She never did get to whack him—hip and thigh, as the Bible would have it. It was frustrating, it was tiring and it was totally unsatisfactory!

Abby opened one eye and looked out of the window at a weak sun trying to rise over the hills of Martha's Vineyard island. Time to get up, she grumbled to herself. Her sheets were all in twisted skeins around her legs. She had to unwind them before she could set a foot on the floor.

If I don't get up and make a real breakfast he's going to make some of those peanut butter and jelly sand-

wiches he threatened me with last night. And that, my
girl, is something up with which you shall not put! she
told herself.

She swung herself up out of the bed, sleepily staggered over to the window, raised the blind and threw the
window open. There was a fine wind coming in from
the east, bringing with it the flavor of sea and shore and
all the world of fishing. Gulls haunted the stern of one
of the passenger ferries which ploughed the waters north
of them from Woods Hole to Martha's Vineyard and
back again. Here and back and the birds followed along,
having learned long ago that the best of food came off
the stern of one of these vessels after the breakfast or
dinner meals.

Resolving to get going, Abby looked around her, found
her robe and slippers, gathered up her underclothes, and
padded down to the ornate bathroom. There was not a
sign of life from either of the other two bedrooms. Which
is just as well, she told herself. The last thing I need is
to have two strange men following me around while I'm
showering.

So she went as quietly as possible into the bathroom
and started the shower. The quick response of the electric
generator soon gave her hot water with enough to spare.
She soaked under the pleasure of it and then was reminded by a movement outside the bathroom door that
her time was fast fleeing. She stepped out, dried off,
climbed into her undies and slipped into a pair of blue
jeans and a light yellow blouse. Her hair was more than
she could handle so she left it the way it was. Raggedy
Ann, she told herself and laughed. Raggedy Ann looking
for Raggedy Andy. Stop this, Abigail, she chided herself.
There is more to this whole family setup than you know.
Something is seriously wrong and you may not wish to
be dragged into this whole mess. But a little voice in her

subconscious whispered that if there was trouble ahead little Abby Spencer would be among the first to offer to help. She blamed her mother for this affliction of hers—offering to help. Along with the ladylike lessons, her mother had been, and still was, big on simple kindness and the proverbial helping hand.

She picked up her night things and went out into the hall again. Her dog was waiting with her yellow tennis ball clenched between her teeth.

"Come on, girl," she said softly. "Downstairs. Breakfast. If you don't put that darn ball away you won't eat."

Breakfast—that was the magic word. The dog lifted up her ears, hiked herself up to her feet and raced, if that was a word that could be used about Cleo, to the head of the stairs. She turned, looking for praise. Her ball dropped out of her mouth and went merrily bouncing down the dark stairs. They both could hear the ball bouncing at least partway down the staircase. They made their way down, with Abby holding tightly on to the banister on one side, and Cleo's collar on the other. Neither she nor Cleo could find the yellow ball. Cleo sat down at the foot of the stairs and mourned.

"I didn't throw it," Abby said. "Don't expect me to go fetch it for you. Come on."

Her "woman's best friend" offered a little growl. Abby stamped her foot on the dull linoleum. Complaining was acceptable; threatening was prohibited. They both knew the rules, but Cleo was standing up for her own principles.

"Breakfast," Abby announced heartily. Cleo wavered. Caught between principle and practicality, the dog gave up and followed her mistress down the hall. It had been almost twenty-four hours since Cleo had eaten and any word having to do with food was welcome and eagerly anticipated.

Breakfast? Abby asked herself as she led the way down to the kitchen. What in the world have we got to eat?

There had been something nagging her all night, despite the bad dream with Selby Farnsworth. She had brought enough food for herself to last ten days. There certainly wasn't enough to last for three weeks, especially for three people. Unless there was some way to call for a boat, the food was going to be getting scarce after a few days. But she'd keep her secret for at least a couple of days.

There was a propane refrigerator in the far corner of the kitchen, fed through a flexible tube that ran out to the back of the house. When she had first come in the day before, she had packed all her perishables in it, fired the cooling pilot light and then had gone off and forgotten it.

Now she opened the door carefully. A blast of cold air struck her face. Inventory: two dozen eggs, a rasher of bacon, sausages galore, bread for toasting. That last was a problem. The only way she could make toast was over the flames in the fireplace, and that fire was now only a glowing ember or two. After a ten-minute struggle Abby gave up.

She had been a girl scout, but as she recalled she had only been awarded the badge for sewing, and had to get her mother to sew it on for her. While she pondered on the problem of toast, Harry wandered into the kitchen. He looked hungry and just a little intimidated by the presence of Cleo. Abby smiled at him because he was really just a little boy. He was in the process of growing in his adult teeth; there were a few missing from the line up. There has to be a way to get on his good side, she told herself. With all of the training I've had there must be something I can try.

"Are you gonna cook breakfast?" Harry asked. "Have you fed the dog? She won't eat me, will she?"

"Cleo?" Abby answered. "My dog never eats my friends. She only eats people who aren't my friends. She and I have an agreement on that subject. But I'm glad you reminded me. I haven't fed her this morning and she probably is hungry."

Harry shrugged his shoulders, stubbed his toe on a worn section of the linoleum and looked up at her with a wicked little gleam in his eyes. "Could I be a friend of yours? Can I help feed her?"

"Well," Abby drawled it out, "perhaps, maybe. It would depend."

"Depend on what?"

"Well, it depends on how you treat me. Friends treat friends nicely. You haven't been that nice to me so far. Are you going to be friendly to me? We have to work through the friend part first and then we'll talk about you feeding her."

"I don't mind," the boy said. "I ain't scared of that." He had both hands behind his back and he was very slowly moving across the carpet toward her, very, very slowly.

Cleo watched him carefully. As he got close enough to be within her attack range she came up to a half crouch and growled a little. Harry came to a complete stop and the look he gave to Abby was one of, You told me it was okay, so what did I do wrong? Abby smiled and reached out to pat the old dog on the head. "That's enough, Cleo. That's enough. This is a friend. Now, Harry, hold out one hand in front of her nose. Don't touch her."

The boy gulped and then carefully, as if he were guarding a treasure, moved his left hand from behind his back. It was still clutched in a fist and he extended it slowly in the dog's direction. Cleo came all the way to her feet, looked up at her mistress and then back at the boy. She took a couple of sniffs at the proffered hand and after a moment the old collie licked the knuckles.

"There you are," Abby said. "You have been identified as a friend of mine, which makes you a friend of Cleo's. Okay?"

"I suppose you and me can be friends. Are you gonna cook breakfast or feed Cleo first?"

"I suppose I could start our breakfast if you'll go upstairs to my bedroom and get her bag of food. Once you get it down here, you can put some in a bowl for her along with some water. You will have helped to feed her at that point and you will have become one of Cleo's best friends. She loves anyone who feeds her. The quickest way to Cleo's heart is through her stomach."

She set the bread aside while Harry clumped up the stairs and she reached for the eggs. The propane stove chirped on without a bit of trouble. In a moment or two she constructed a fine bunch of fried eggs, sunny side up. Just enough, she thought to herself, and turned around with the platter in both hands, moving in the direction of the kitchen table.

She hadn't heard Harry come back down the stairs so she was startled when she saw a different male face sitting at the breakfast table, beaming at her and her dish of eggs. She stopped with one foot still in the air. "I didn't hear you come in," she said suspiciously.

"No," he admitted. There was a very insincere grin on his face. "No, I was afraid that if I made a noise you might be surprised and drop something. My, that looks nice."

"If she dropped the plate then we don't get anything nice to eat," the boy said as he came back into the kitchen with the bag of dog food.

"I've got to teach you better, boy," his father grumbled. "Don't play Abraham Lincoln. You don't have to be all *that* honest."

"Yes, he does," Abby insisted. "And, besides, after he's finished feeding the dog, there's just enough food here for Harry and me."

She put the platter down in front of her own space, shoveled an egg and a sausage onto the boy's plate and put it at the open space at the table. Harry was very busily filling the bowls Abby had found with dog food and water. He was looking very serious about this task and was very gratified when Cleo shouldered him out of the way to get at *her* food. All of the good food smells had been driving her crazy and she was *hungry!*

"I guess that means that she likes me, huh?" It sounded to Abby as if Harry Farnsworth needed someone to approve of his actions. He needed to be praised.

"Yes. I guess that means that you are one of the top people on Cleo's list of friends and you did that very well. I didn't realize that the bag was so big. How did you get it down the stairs?"

"I just bumped it down the stairs," Harry semi-bragged. He had done something good and she had noticed. She was someone he liked for some reason. The fact that she had a dog was a big point in her favor, but he liked her anyway.

"Then why don't you sit down and eat your breakfast while it's hot?" She turned around and went back to the frying pan, which was still sizzling with bacon. By the time she had settled that and had returned to the table again, all the rest of the food had disappeared.

"Which one of you?" she said, eyeing them both disgustedly. "Which one of you ate my breakfast?"

"Not me," the boy said. "I wouldn't do a thing like that." He ducked his head so that he would not be looking at his father.

"Well," Selby said, "if he's innocent, and you're innocent, I guess I'm the guilty party."

"You've got a nerve," she growled at him. "You threaten me with a peanut butter sandwich and now you expect me to cook something deliciously delightful for your breakfast?"

"That is exactly what I hoped for," he said, and made no attempt to hide the twinkle in those big brown eyes.

"I have a good mind," she told him, her green eyes sparking, "to dispossess you right this minute. You've got enough nerve to——"

"Watch the bacon," Harry yelled at them both. Abby wheeled around. She had spooned the rest of the bacon to the top of the chopping board to let it drain off. While the pair of them were arguing, Cleo had slithered by them, flat on her stomach, and then leaped up to seize the bacon and the paper on which it was drying.

Dog food was fine for those rainy days when there was nothing around to scrounge, but the aroma of bacon was a siren call to Cleo. If there was bacon around and no one was watching, then she would make a try for it. The dog was making no effort to share. She saw it as only right that she be entitled to anything she could snatch—and bacon was fair game. Four big gulps and it was all gone. Abby, hands on hips, turned to search the two innocent faces. "Why is it," she asked the world around her, "that I'm beginning to feel put upon?" She could feel the color of anger as it flashed up into her cheeks. Anger, and something else she had learned in her high school drama club, was helping her put color

in her face. How to cry without even trying. And Abby
Spencer was very good at it. Very good indeed. She was
counting on it to make a very big impression.

She managed to pull one chair away from the table.
Her tall figure collapsed into it for a moment, and then
she straightened her back and closed her eyes. Think
sadness, she commanded. Scenes flashed in front of her
eyes, but she dispatched them one after another. Finally
she found the one she wanted. She pictured herself
standing on the hillside on grandfather's farm, on the
warm autumn day when her pony had broken its leg and
had to be put down.

The scene solidified. She could remember every sound,
every wind-blown smell, the soft muttering of the sheep.
And then the sound of the gun. Abby held that sound
close to her heart. The tears began. Solemn, quiet tears
oozing up from under her eyelids, and running down
her cheeks, one or two at a time, and then in full flood.

"Now look what you done," the boy said fiercely.

"Pay it no mind," his father said. "Women cry for
no reason at all."

"She had a reason," the boy snapped. "I've told you
before. This is a nice one, and you made her cry. Why?"

"Maybe you're right, Harry. I didn't think she'd cry.
Let me see if I can stop the tears."

"You'd better," the boy threatened.

Abby, doing her best to keep the tears rolling, was
startled to hear the boy crying as well. The kitchen door
slammed as Harry ran out, leaving her alone with Selby.
Not exactly what I planned, Abby told herself. She threw
in a couple of additional sobs.

There was movement, and a strong arm came around
her shoulders. She cracked one eyelid. Selby was kneeling
at her side, trying to get a big handkerchief out of his

pocket. "I don't understand," he murmured. "A girl as big as you are, crying?"

I'll show you *big*, she thought as she turned up the sobs and slumped over, resting all of her hundred and thirty-five-pound weight against him. It took but a moment for her to realize she had made a terrible mistake. He *liked* having her lean on him. He especially liked the softness of her full breast, falling haphazardly into the cup of his hand.

"Don't." She struggled to sit up, but the cold intervention of the world around her ruined her comfort. With a little gasp she fell back into his arms. "Don't," she repeated in a soft, pleading whisper.

"Don't?" He pulled her closer, gently massaging her breast, and then said, "Oh. You mean this?" His right hand pulled her up, his left hand continued to gently support her breast.

"I mean don't!" This time indignantly. She wrenched herself away from him. His right hand came loose. His left hand seemed to twitch for a moment, and then he helped her to stand. She was still quivering. She clutched her fists and thrust them down along the seams of her jeans. Her whole body shook, until the muscle tension brought her under control.

"Don't you ever touch me like that again," she spat.

He held his hand up before him, still flexing the fingers. "It was delightful," he announced.

"I didn't enjoy it," she lied. She might have said more, but Harry came back into the room. There was a moment or two of silence and then Harry said, "I had enough breakfast for the day. Now what am I gonna do?"

His father looked at him seriously, as if he was debating the subject. "Well," Selby said, "I know what I've got to do. I've got to redo those pages you used to color on yesterday. Maybe Abby can think of something for you both to do."

"Why should I be the one to come up with entertainment ideas? I have work to do too, you know. Very important work!"

Selby looked over at her, and there was a tug at the corner of his mouth, as if he couldn't resist laughing, but had to. "Yes. But we have a small problem," he said. "Someone has to entertain Harry and I've got a living to make. I'm sure you could fit child care into your schedule."

"Oh? What gave you that misguided idea?" Abby pounced on his last statement. She might not be a rabid feminist but she did hold that talent and drive were neither gender-oriented nor segregated. Women did not have to be the child tenders. But the look on Harry's face soon shut her up. He looked as if he had heard this argument about who was going to look after him before and it made him feel like a package no one wanted.

"I'll tell you what, nobody has to entertain me. I'll go fishing by myself. You two can work all you want. Don't think about me. I'll go fishing!" With that Harry ran out of the kitchen with a very set look on his face.

Abby slumped back in her chair and glared at Selby. "You brought the kid out to this island. Why did you do that if you weren't going to spend time with him?"

"I spent all day yesterday with him," Selby flashed at her.

"Do you honestly think that one day is enough? What did you do for the first three weeks you were here?"

"We did things together," Selby defended himself. "It's different for men. We don't have to be together all the hours of the day. And, besides, Harry is getting to be a big boy and big boys like to investigate on their own."

"If you both have been here three weeks then Harry must know the island very well. There's not that much of it to investigate." Abby was getting more and more angry on Harry's behalf with this whole conversation.

Stop it, she told herself, this is not helping anything and you know you want to help.

"I suppose I could start my work tomorrow. I'll go fishing with Harry," Abby said after she had mastered her anger.

"That'll be nice," Selby said, looking as if he had been giving himself instructions to calm down. "Especially considering the fact that Harry doesn't know anything about fishing. If you two catch something it would enlarge our food supply. Harry and I both love fried fish."

"I have always hated fried fish," Abby said, "and I don't see any reason why——" And she stopped at that point. *Sucker*, she told herself. He's just trying to cajole you into looking after the boy full-time. His father was staring at her with a look that said, Of course you will. Abby felt stalled between announcing, "The hell you say," or going along with the game to see what else might develop. She was fairly sure, however, what was going to develop and that it would involve Harry and herself doing things together. Her *own* work would suffer. Her editor would want her head on a pike. Oh, well, in for a penny.

"Yes," she finally said, "Harry and I will go fishing. What are you going to be doing?"

"Well," he said, "I have a great deal of work to do. I need to rewrite some pages that were lost to the world of adolescent art and they have to be replaced so that I can finish this paper."

"I heard you last night," Abby chipped in. "Is this going to be a long paper? What are you writing? Do you think it will ever be published?"

"Published? Please—I'm writing something for a legal case I'm working on. Well, it's a very long argument and I have to keep at it, so I'll put my grind to the nosestone while you two have all the fun in the world."

"Yes, I can bet you will," Abby said sarcastically. "Put your nose to the grindstone, I mean." Another discouraged sigh. "I don't suppose you would consider that I have a great deal of work to do myself?"

He waved her off. "Surely not as important as mine, my dear." There was a suave tone in his voice. Like a traveling salesman, Abby thought. He'd make a good Hellfire and Damnation preacher. Or perhaps a politician—no, nothing *that* bad. Like all non-politicians in Washington, Abby could be either a devoted follower, or a member of a "hate" group. Usually she fitted under the latter label.

"And just what," Abby said indignantly, "do you suppose will happen to all the work that I brought with me? I have to get it done. There's a deadline and I need peace and quiet."

"Oh, you don't need that much time," Selby said. "Anyone of your caliber, any good red-blooded American woman can do this kind of thing easily. Besides, that's what New Englanders do best, isn't it, fishing?"

"Let me remind you," Abby said very firmly, "that I come from Washington, D.C., not New England."

"Oh, that slipped my mind," Selby said. "Slipped my ever-loving mind. My apologies. But you will take the boy fishing."

"I will take the boy fishing. I said so once before. We will be back at noontime. You will make the lunch. It will not be peanut butter sandwiches. And you will look around for Cleo's ball. She'll go whompers if we can't find it."

"Did you hear that, Harry?" the man said loudly.

"Yeah, I heard it." A tearstained Harry came into the room. "I wasn't gonna go until I got Cleo to come with me."

"A boy and his dog," Selby said softly. "I remember those days with my dog Sam."

There was a look on his face that was at odds with the impression Abby had been forming of him. It looked as if he cared about his son and just didn't know how to go about connecting with him. "It will not be peanut butter sandwiches, and I must find Cleo's ball. This lady must have been a drill sergeant."

"I heard it," the boy said. "I hope—I hope it works out right. I think the ball might taste better than the peanut butter. But I do want to go fishing."

"Well, then," Abby said, "what we need are a couple of fishing poles, some bait—did you bring any bait, either of you?"

"Not me," Selby said. "What is it, this bait business?"

"Oh, my Lord." Abby sighed as she pushed her chair away from the table. "I am very suspicious, Mr. Farnsworth. Sometimes you seem to know everything in the world and sometimes you don't seem to know anything at all."

"Ah. I have had many women tell me that," Selby said. "It's a failure in my system some place. Harry, all the fishing gear is out in that hut behind the house. Do you want to go get it?"

The little boy jumped up, wide-eyed, expectant, and went out as fast as his legs could take him.

"Now, what is all this?" Abby said. "Some sort of condition that you are setting?"

"Sit down, Abby," he said. "There's something I need to talk to you about."

"I'm not sure there is anything I need to hear from you."

"Abigail, I want to talk to you about Harry."

"You want to talk to me about Harry? About how he behaved last night? About how he went off to bed all by himself? How there was not an adult in sight to tuck him in, wish him well, tell him a story? Is that what you wanted to talk to me about?"

"Lord, I never imagined all that," Selby said. "And yes, that is partly what I wanted to talk to you about. It's a difficult thing—a little boy who can't sleep through the night. Who wakes up crying as he goes around the house looking for——"

"Looking for what?" Abby interrupted.

"Looking for his mother," Selby said. "I want to thank you for the kindness and consideration you showed last night and I want to thank you for the future kindness I am sure you will show him. I have a troubled little boy and I don't know everything there is to know about handling him. He was given to his mother by the courts after our divorce five years ago. After a long struggle I've finally been given visitation rights. I've only a short time to get to know the boy—and I'm desperate. Will you help?"

And with a plea like that, Abby told herself, how could I not?

CHAPTER THREE

ABBY pushed her chair back again and stood up.

"You don't have to know anything much about raising children," she said. "What you have to do is love him and show it. You have to give him some prime-time acceptance. You have to be with him when he needs you. We used to call that 'parenting' in the old days. I don't suppose you know much about that?"

"Well, that's true," he said. "I don't know much about parenting. That's all it takes? Love? Kindness?"

"TLC," Abby said. "Tender loving care. Well, now. While we're gone, you might perhaps do the dishes. Wash the pots, clean the sink and generally look over the house. We'll be back soon."

"What a bargainer you are," he said, but there was a smile hiding in back of his voice. "All this just for a fishing trip?"

"All this *because* of a fishing trip," she said firmly. "Now don't stand around. Get whistling."

"Wait just a darn minute," he objected. "You are going to walk off with my son to go fishing and have all that fun, and me, I have to just stand around here and imagine what I am supposed to do?"

"What you imagine? I was under the impression you couldn't come because of a case you have to finish preparing," Abby queried as she started to walk by him. "Tender loving care, that's all you need—oh, and a washcloth to get the dirt off him occasionally."

"Hey, wait a minute," he said. "Tender loving care— does that include——?"

45

By this time, Abby was all the way past him, and suddenly his long arm came around her, pulled her back until she was facing him.

"What is it that you want?" she said, stringing the words out harshly.

"I want a sample, a bit of instruction," he said. There was a guileless look on his face, as if he was the perfectly innocent victim of all the world's harsh ways.

"A bit of instruction?" she asked. "What in the world are you talking about? What's so hard about caring for Harry?"

"Well, I know the first part," he said. "I suppose you know the last. It goes like this." Both his arms tightened around her, holding her helplessly against him. One of his hands came free and a finger went under her chin, tilting it upward. He bent farther and touched her lips with his, just a gentle touch.

"Tender loving care," he said, almost in a whisper.

"Yes," Abby said, "but I——"

"I know," he said. "Hang on. I'll get it right this time."

He bent to kiss her. The world seemed to fall quiet all around them, as if they were at the dead center of a hurricane, in the eye. She felt she had complete control of her world, except that nothing was paying any attention to her needs. She thought to scream for help, but she was rolled up in the warm, peaceful sharing of herself. When he finally broke contact all that warmth and peace faded away. She moaned for its recall, without success.

"Hey, I've got a talent for kissing, haven't I?" he said cheerfully.

"I don't know what you've got," Abby said, trying to appear angry as she pushed away from him. "It may be smallpox, for all I know. But I don't want to catch any more of it. Goodbye, Mr. Farnsworth." She stomped out of the kitchen and let the swinging door slam behind her.

Behind her, in the kitchen, Selby Farnsworth stood with a smile on his face. "Tender loving care," he said to anyone who wanted to listen. He rocked back and forth on his heels for a moment and shoved his hands into his pockets. There was a bemused expression on his face. Something had happened that he hadn't expected. He was a man with a great deal of experience—with women. But just this quick touching of lips with *this* woman had jolted him out of control. He shook his head and headed for the stairs, muttering, "Good Lord," as he did so.

Outside on the porch Abby met the boy, who was loaded with equipment. They divided the load and started off for the north end of the island, where a pier projected out into Buzzard's Bay.

"Was you kissin' my dad?" the boy asked when they were about twenty feet away from the house.

"Not exactly," Abby replied. "I wasn't kissing him, he was kissing me. What else would you like to ask?"

"Um—since you asked, are you married or something, like going around with some other guy, or like that? I don't want my dad mixed up with things like that. He ain't too smart about women."

"But you are?" she teased. He glared up at her. "No, I'm not any of those things."

He gave a massive sigh, almost as if he had been holding his breath. He reached out and tentatively touched her hand, and then, hoping to distract her, asked, "Is this where we're gonna fish?"

"No. At the end of the island," Abby said. "Around the other side of this hill, where the pier is. You remember where the little boat with the yellow stripe was tied up?"

"Uh-oh," the boy said. "You ain't forgot that yet?"

"No," she said, "I ain't forgot that yet. And it may be a long, long time before I do. But that's where we're going to go fishing. Out at the end of the pier is the only place where we can put a line in the deep water. Bluefish and tautog are about the only fish running now."

"How do you know all that? You must be awful smart."

"Yeah, smart," she said, chuckling. "When I rented the boat over at Woods Hole I asked the manager."

"That's smart," he told her.

"All right. Now we have to find something we can use for bait. Or do you have some bait in your box?"

"Have any bait?" the boy repeated. "I don't got no bait. I don't even know what bait is."

"Holy crow," Abby said. "You've really never been fishing before?"

"Not never."

"Your daddy never took you fishing before?"

"Not never."

"Okay. I brought a can of bait with me, but it's gone floating away in the——"

"In the little yellow boat," the boy interrupted mournfully.

Abby flashed him a wide grin. "That's no major crime," she told him. "C'mon."

Down at the corner of the island where once her uncle had grown potatoes there was a turned-over area which might make easy digging.

"Dig here," said Abby. "You've got the shovel."

"I—yes," the boy said. He took the little collapsible shovel, opened it up and shoved the blade as deeply into the earth as he could. The shovel sank an inch or two, then stopped. He used both hands on the handle, then stepped with all his weight on the shovel's haft. It didn't go very much deeper. He pulled it out and gave it another try. He turned around toward Abby and shrugged his shoulders. "I don't think I can dig any holes here," he said.

"No," Abby said, "I can see that. What we need is a big strong man like your father. Barring that, maybe a relatively weak young lady like me, huh?"

"I go along with that," Harry agreed. "What are you going to do?"

Abby showed him. She slammed the point of the spade into the dirt, balanced herself, stepped onto the haft, and bounced a couple of times. The blade of the shovel sank almost out of sight.

"Now," she said, "you help. We pull, we turn over the earth and if we are lucky there will be worms."

They weren't lucky.

"Oh, boy," Abby said some ten minutes later. "You know, I wish we had known yesterday that you wanted to go fishing today. The time to catch worms is just at dawn or nightfall when the earth is all covered with dew and the worms come up. They hide from the light of day."

"What are they lookin' for?" the boy asked. "The early bird?"

"Wise guy. There's something to be learned from birds and worms, young man," Abby said. "Tell you what we'll do, though. With no live bait, the only thing we could expect to catch is a dumb fish. Let's try a piece of bread." She whipped out of her pocket two slices of the old loaf of bread that was hiding in the corner of the kitchen. It was dry and mildewed, but perhaps the fish wouldn't notice.

"You mean to tell me that fishes eat bread?" Harry asked. There was a distinct undertone of, I don't believe this one, in his voice. She smiled at him.

They walked over to the base of the pier. "What's that?" he asked excitedly.

"That's a flagpole," she returned. "My great-uncle Theodore was a soldier in the First World War. When he was in residence on the island he would raise the flag every morning and——"

"And fire the cannon? Can I——?"

"And fire the cannon," she continued, "and no, you can't fire it." 'It" was a small saluting cannon, with a black iron tube. It was mounted on a gray wood cradle and could be breech-loaded. "It's not a toy," she said. "Come on now."

He came reluctantly, looking over his shoulder at the cannon. At the far end of the pier she gave him a demonstration on how to bait the hook. Breaking off a hunk of the bread, she tapped it gently until it was fixed on her hook.

"Now the thing you have to watch," she said, "is that you and I keep separate from the hook and the fish. If we get the hook stuck in us, we're in a lot of trouble. You got that?"

"I got that."

Just across the way they could see people on Naushon Island, the larger of the Elizabeth Islands, going about the same thing they were, throwing a fishing line in the water. And there ahead of them, up the channel out of Woods Hole, came the Martha's Vineyard motor vessel. It chugged along at flank speed, puffing as if it was already tired. A deckload of tourists waved as they went by.

Abby settled herself down, her back against one of the bollards. Harry watched for a minute, and followed suit. "You know what?" he asked.

"No, what?"

"If there was a nice lady like you around when I grow up, I might even of married her."

"Well, thank you," Abby returned. "I think."

Selby Farnsworth watched them from the upstairs window, the one on the opposite end of the house to the bathroom. They seemed to get along well. They disappeared from his sight when they went to dig worms but were back in view again as they walked out to the end of the long wharf and sat down together, fishing.

They looked so right together, this woman and his son. Selby continued to watch the pair of them as they sat on the dock fishing, talking and laughing. I brought Harry here, he thought, so I could try and understand my son better. I thought that just the two of us could become more friendly. I haven't seen much of him lately with his school and my work, but that's no excuse, is it? When his mother brought him back I thought that Harry and I could get along very well without women. We were doing all right, for a while. The counselor I've been taking Harry to thought we had conquered these nightmares. But Abby shows up, and—bang!—Harry has nightmares again. After all this time of disliking women and accusing all of them of behavior like my ex-wife's, I think we may have found the one that could help both of us. Look at him smile at her. I don't think I've seen such a whole-hearted grin on his face for months. But I'm not rushing into any relationship just for Harry. I'm going to have to be logical and very, very careful.

She's such fun to kiss. Now that's logical. She's the right height. I don't have to bend down too far to kiss her. She is definitely the right shape. His left hand curled as if he could still feel the softness of her breast and he missed the weight on his palm. Harry likes her. I have never seen him warm so quickly to anyone in his life. She seems to like him and she seems to care.

Who is she? What is she doing here? Why is she here—now? Curiosity had always been one of Selby's major traits and he was now standing outside her door. It was open. He took a step inside, feeling like a burglar. Everything was a mess. She had made no attempt to make her bed, nor straighten anything out. Her semi-transparent nightgown hung over the foot of the bed and he could instantly see her in it—in his mind, that was. Daydreaming. "Lord, if I keep on like this," he said aloud, "I'm really gonna lose control."

He made an effort and pushed himself away to walk down the hall. His own room was spartan; everything was immaculate. It looked as if some soldier back from the wars had been stationed here. And all he could think of was, Wow, if my mother could only see me now. But, of course, that was all something to be thought of later.

He went over to his cupboard, reached up on the top shelf and pulled down a box which contained his portable battery-operated cellular telephone.

Now I hope the devil that Abby never finds out, he told himself, as he sat down on the bed and plugged in the little machine. It took some time for the call to go through. In fact, he had to make an assisted call in the end. It wasn't because he was in such a far-off place. There were telephone terminals for radio telephones located in Falmouth and Hyannis, as well as Woods Hole. All three cities could be seen directly across the straits from his room.

Eventually he got the call through. He felt more relaxed when the expected voice answered.

"Congressman Farnsworth's office," his secretary, Peggy Fornat, answered. "May I help you?"

"Peg," he said, "it's me."

"Oh, my God," she said, "don't talk too loud."

"What's the matter?"

"You can't imagine," Peggy said, her voice pitched a little higher than normal. "The place is loaded with rumors. Someone has started the story that you are out in the boonies with the girl of the day, living it up. And the House Whip has been down here twice, demanding that I call you in."

"I understand about the Whip," he said. "He wants me on the floor when the agriculture bill comes up. But I don't understand about the rumor. Why now?"

"I'm not sure," Peggy said. His ears almost automatically came to attention. Peg had been secretary to a long line of congressmen. She had, gossip said, a pipeline into every office and cubbyhole on the Hill. "But how about your former wife? She's in town. Yes, she even stopped by here to find out if I had an address for you. No, she didn't say what she wanted, but just think, Congressman. Suppose the Whip hears the rumor and believes it. You were out playing tag with some broad when he needs your vote on the floor?"

"I know," he said, groaning. "My name would be mud with the party. I'd lose every good assignment I ever had or had even wanted. Look, Peggy. This is important. I can't come in tomorrow, the way I planned."

"It's your funeral," his secretary commented. "And what am I supposed to do?"

"Stall, Peggy, darling. And I want you to do something else for me. I had arranged with the Guiness Boat Company over in Hyannis to come over and pick me up tomorrow morning. I don't want that to happen. I want you to call ahead and see if you can postpone it at least for another week." He winced at his secretary's groan. "I have something going here and I think it will help Harry."

"Aha," said Peggy. "Something going, huh? I just hope that it is for Harry's sake because we can't forget, chum, this is the year of sweet peace and harmony in Congress. Too many people have been found with someone else's wife in tow. You could get in a lot of trouble if they pick you up with the wrong little bird in your nest."

"Oh, come on, Peg," he said. "Just see that the call is made. All right? And you don't have any idea where I am but I'll contact you next week. Okay?"

"Okay. I still don't understand why you haven't told anyone else about Harry and his problems. That should be worth all kinds of sympathy votes. You know, the great congressional parent going overboard for his son. Oh, Lord, here comes your wife again," Peggy said. "Goodbye." And she hung up.

Selby looked around his room. Everything neat, everything precise, a reminder of his military days. Just the way I like it, he mused. Everything tied up with that beautiful girl out on the pier. And my former wife? What in the world can she be after?

Of course, there was no way in the world to find out without asking. And that he was not going to do. He carefully repacked his box, put his telephone away, covered it over with a spare blanket, and sat down to work on his half-finished novel.

About an hour later he heard voices. He hurriedly covered his machine and walked back down the hall. The pair of them, Abby and Harry, were walking back up the hill, holding hands, no less! That startled him.

He had never found a woman whom Harry would hold hands with, not even his own mother.

He got over to the head of the stairs without any trouble but darkness still covered the stairwell. He started down cautiously. Abby and his son were at the door and as the boy opened it and came in he yelled, "Dad, have you found Cleo's ball cuz we caught a fish."

Striding down the stairs, he had to chuckle.

"No, I haven't," he called. "I haven't yet——" At that moment he found the ball. In the darkness his left foot landed on top of it. The ball cheerily spurted away from him. For a majestic moment Selby wavered, and then he too bounced down several sets of stairs, perhaps not so cheerfully as had the little ball. His fundament made a painful contact with three sets of risers before he came to a halt. And to add insult to injury the ball bounced over his head and landed in his outstretched hands.

By that time, Harry had rushed over to the bottom of the stairs. Abby tagged along behind him. "Did you hurt yourself?" the lad asked.

"Not really, son. I was searching for Cleo's ball. This is the only way to do it. It's called stair-sliding."

"And did you find it?"

"Like the Northwest Mounted Police," he said solemnly. "We always get our man—er—I mean the ball."

"See there?" The boy turned eagerly toward Abby. "My dad can do *anything*!"

"I can see he can," Abby said. "If we had taken him fishing I'm sure we would have caught something bigger than this."

Selby struggled to his feet, paying no attention to the pains that rose with him. Heroism is a prideful thing, he reminded himself as he used the banister for support.

"That's a pretty big fish. What kind is it?" he asked.

"It's a bluefish and we caught it using bread. Ain't that strange? But Abby says that bluefish only go for bread so it was a good thing that we didn't find no worms." Harry was excited and would have kept on talking had he not run out of breath.

"See, Dad, Abby knows everything about fishing! You should have come!"

"You really should," Abby said. "Maybe if you come next time we could catch a whale. I think that this bluefish should feed us for one meal. Now all we have to worry about, Harry, is how your father is going to cook the darn thing. Maybe if you're really lucky he'll show you how to clean it, too."

"Isn't it the fisherperson's duty to clean the catch?" Selby said with exaggerated wincing to make Harry laugh.

"Not this fisherwoman. I belong to a very strong union and I'm forbidden to clean fish." Abby said all of this with a perfectly straight face but she was thinking that just maybe Selby did care for Harry.

"Crow," he said somberly. "I'm sure I could fix myself a good dish of crow for my lunch. I suppose that I'll have to think of something for the two of you. Come on, Harry, let's go to the kitchen and slave over a hot stove."

She grinned at him, offered a little curtsy, and headed up the staircase. "Just remember, no fried fish!"

"I don't understand women," little Harry said.

"Yes, you're right," his father said. "I have the same problem myself."

CHAPTER FOUR

THEY were all sitting at the dinner table at five o'clock that night. "This is a lovely meal," Abby said. "I don't know when I've had better. So shall I add cooking to your numerous other qualifications, Selby?"

The little boy grinned at her from across the table. "My dad can do anything," he said.

"How about that?" his father said, smiling. "Unsolicited testimonials."

"Well deserved. What type of meat is this?"

"Coney," Selby reported. "A local meat, available from time to time."

"Rabbit," Harry interjected. "Wild rabbit."

Abby struggled with her stomach. It had all tasted so good, but as a child she had kept two pet rabbits, and her memory was strong. She grounded her spoon and coughed, hoping that the conversation would go away. But she had no such luck.

"There are a couple of dozen rabbits on the island," Selby continued. "I was teaching Harry how to make traps, and we managed to catch a couple."

"I skinned the second one," Harry said. "My dad showed me how."

By this time Abby had found a handkerchief in the pocket of her jeans. She pulled it out and held it over her mouth. Her two male companions, insensitive to her problem, ploughed merrily ahead in a two-way discussion about how exactly such things were done.

"My dad taught me," Selby said. "I'm just passing the knowledge along."

There was a two-second pause. Abby jumped into it with both feet. "I think Cleo needs to have a run outside. Harry, why don't you go along and play ball with her?"

The boy turned to her with a puzzled expression on his face. "I never played ball with a dog."

"It's easy. All you have to do is take her yellow ball with you. She'll follow along. Outside, you throw the ball and she'll fetch it. She loves the game."

"Yes, go ahead," his father agreed. "It'll do you both good to have a little exercise. But you be darned sure you keep away from the water, son."

The boy slid out of his chair and dashed for the door. Cleo trailed after him.

"More coffee?" Abby offered. He nodded and held out his mug to be filled. She poured gracefully from the heavy pot. He tipped a salute to her with his mug.

"You're a strange pair, you and your son," she commented as she watched him sip the brew. There was something about his eyebrows. They extended almost completely across the bridge of his nose. The one over his right eye had a couple of white hairs sticking straight up. She hadn't noticed it before. "The sign of Lucifer?" she asked, gesturing.

He grinned again, and smoothed the eyebrow down with one finger. It sprang up almost immediately. "A family heritage. Just like my father. And, come to think of it, my grandfather too. You think there's something devilish about us?"

Abby passed up a comment. There was another pregnant pause. Abby could hear Harry's shrill cheers from outside the house, punctuated by an occasional bark from Cleo. "Why," she asked, "do I get the feeling that this is all new to Harry?"

He grounded his mug and drummed a couple of fingers on the table, as if trying to come to some decision. "It is," he said. "Harry——" He paused and drummed his fingers again. "Well, that's not starting off right. None of what's happened has been Harry's fault. I don't know if you would want to hear it all."

"Try me." She put both elbows on the table and rested her chin between her hands.

"We," he started over again, "my former wife and I—we had a particularly nasty separation. I think we both tried to use Harry as a whipping boy. But it's been only lately that I've secured visitation rights." He paused for a moment, his eyes wandering around the room as if to concentrate on what he meant to say next. "I've been too damn busy, and that spells trouble in a one-parent family. That's the main reason for this trip. I wanted a chance to show my boy what it means to be a man."

"He learns fast."

"Yes, he does that. Maybe too fast. Did I tell you he's a brilliant boy? His Intelligence Quotient is so high I feel sort of humble. He's a whiz in maths."

"Nothing wrong with that," Abby commented.

"Plenty's wrong with that," Selby said, and slammed his fist down on the table. "He knows all about figures, and nothing at all about how to be a normal boy. On top of that, although he knows that his mother can't stand him, he's set and determined to bring us back together again."

"Is that such an impossible thing?"

"Absolutely impossible," he said, and for some reason Abby's heart gave a little skip. A thought came unbidden to her mind. Maybe you could use a substitute? Her tongue struggled with the phrase, and then gave up.

"Why don't we step out into the sunshine?" he suggested. They rose from the table together. "Leave the dishes," he commanded. "Harry and I will do them later."

"I'll go along with that," Abby replied.

They walked out in a companionable silence, holding hands. Abby failed to notice that little contretemps until they had gone around the side of the house. And by that time it seemed to be so pleasant an idea—holding hands, that was—that she couldn't find the strength to object.

There was an old bench set against the back of the house, facing westward. It had room for six. Abby claimed the far corner, tucking her skirts beneath her for fear of splinters. Selby sat down beside her. The bench was automatically too small. His warm thigh pressed against her. Fish or cut bait, Abby's father would have said, but his daughter the Sunday school teacher had no idea how to go about such things.

The rain clouds were fleeing. They left a magnificent rainbow in their wake. "A typical New England storm," he commented. "Threatened on Monday, darkened the sky on Tuesday, finally rained on Wednesday, and blown away on Thursday. Now there is nothing but streamers in the afternoon sun on Friday."

"Lovely," Abby said. "Lovely. I hate to think about it, though, because it's getting so close to winter. Living by the ocean is great just as long as the water is warm. But there will be snow soon enough—and that leaves me cold."

"Oh, please, no puns," Selby said. "What are you going to do this evening?"

"I have some things that I have to read," she told him. "You two will have to get along without me."

"That's all right," he said, "we'll find something to do." Boy and dog had come to join them, both panting, out of breath. "What about it, son? Shall we have a game of chess tonight?"

"Yea," the little boy cried, "I love that. Best three out of five? Abby, are you going to come watch?"

"No, I can't," Abby said. "I've got work to do. Employment, you know. I have to make a buck here and there. Unlike your daddy, who is obviously born rich, I have to work for a living. You both scoot along and I'll catch up with you tomorrow."

She watched them both as they headed back toward the house. Just the viewing relieved a little tension from Abby's heart. Man and boy; all they needed was a woman to be with them. And what woman? What woman? she thought. I wonder if his wife will show up? Maybe he won't need a wife; maybe it's easy enough for them to live with a nanny or somebody's great-aunt, as people did in the old days. If that's the way it turns out— oh, Lord, what a waste.

Now why am I feeling so wrong about something like that? Single-parent families are the thing these days. I have no connection with this man. Surely, this evening was pleasant, holding hands and all. That's not a mark of great esteem, or great love, or even great passion. But if it were to become a passion, wouldn't it be wonderful to be a part of it? She shivered and clasped her arms around herself, even though the weather was warm.

When Abby came downstairs the next morning she was surprised to see Cleo waiting impatiently at the front door. When Harry came in from outside, followed by his father, the dog jumped up on the little boy as if he had suddenly become her best friend. The father was carrying a big cardboard box. It appeared to be heavy.

"Why, you've even stolen my dog," Abby complained, not meaning it at all.

The boy blushed, and shook his head. "No, I ain't stolen her," he said, "I'm just borrowing her for a while.

When we go back home I can't take a dog with me because in our house they don't allow any animals. Ain't that something? I'd like to live out in the country where you could be 'lowed as many pets as you could want. Wouldn't that be nice, Dad?"

"That might be nice, but you know I have to work in the city," his father said.

"Lots of people work in the city. You could drive in or you could fly in or you could quit. After all, you got lots of people who want your job, don't they?"

"Well, thank you very much," his father said sarcastically. "Now hush up, young man. Take your fish out to the kitchen."

"He caught a fish?" Abby asked.

Selby lowered the box. The boy reached in and brought out a four- or five-pound fish, already cleaned and ready for cooking.

"Would you believe that?" Selby said, chuckling.

"Magnificent," Abby said, and then stumbled over her tongue. If it weren't for the boy she would have told him flat out that she didn't believe a bit of it. Although not a fisherman of great renown herself, she knew this was neither tautog nor bluefish. In fact, it looked suspiciously like haddock, fresh off the boat!

Selby was evidently reading her mind. "A fisherman is without honor in his own country," he said. "What would you say if I told you we had to throw two back because they were too small?"

She looked up at him, openmouthed.

"I thought so," he said. "So, young man, take your fish out to the kitchen, put it in the sink, get yourself into the bathroom and wash up. Then we'll see what happens next."

"You betcha," the boy cried as he went racing down the hall toward the kitchen, all exuberance.

"That is something," Abby said cautiously. "Something like Baron Munchausen."

"Baron who?"

"Baron Munchausen, Germany's most famous liar."

Selby looked down at her and smiled. "Ah, but the Baron's long dead. Look at that kid. Filled with exuberance, full of life, everything you could ask for."

She tucked her hand under the bend of his arm and smiled up at him. "I'm not going to fight you," she replied. "It is the way life ought to be lived," she commented. "Give or take a few wild improvisations. We ought to do away with all these books and schemes and lies and crooked congressmen and just raise our kids to be nice and clean and thoughtful——"

"And godly," Selby interrupted. She looked up at him just a little too late. The grimace was just fading, to be replaced by a grin.

Abby was not prepared for battle. One fish story is as good as another, she told herself. My father had fish stories a yard long. But what caused him to wince? Crooked congressmen? She stored her doubts, gave his arm a little squeeze and pushed him in the direction of the kitchen, while she took a detour through the little bathroom under the stairs. Harry was splashing water madly. Some of it was falling on his face and hands, but not much. "Clean," she ordered imperiously, and left him to it.

Out in the kitchen his father had evidently emptied the box, and shoved it under the table. "What we have here," she said as she walked over to the stove, "is a breakfast prepared for three consisting of leftover stew with tomato sauce and cookies. There is no bread and I don't know how to bake. And we're out of orange juice."

"Difficult," Selby agreed.

"They used to be able to make it without ovens in the old days."

"I'm not that old," he said, smiling down at her.

Little Harry came back in at that moment. He had accomplished the impossible, washing only one of his hands. But his hair was slicked down, and he wore a Huck Finn smile. "Did you like my fish?" he asked eagerly.

Abby walked over to the sink, where the fish was draining. "I like it just fine," she told him. "In fact, we'll have it for supper."

"Why," Selby asked of the ceiling, "do I have this suspicion that she really don't mean what she's saying?"

"Just a small doubt," she told him. "First of all, that fish looks so much like a haddock that they could have come from the same school. And haddock don't run in these inshore waters. Secondly, it looks as if it had been professionally cleaned."

"And third?" he demanded. "There has to be a *third*."

"Yes, and third," she continued, "this is the coldest fish I've ever seen. Almost as if it had been iced down, the way professional fishermen would handle it. And——"

"Surely there aren't any more objections?"

"We'll have it for supper," she said. "Now if we only had some vegetables to go with it."

"I don't like vegetables," Harry protested.

"Try the tray in the refrigerator," Selby said.

Abby stared at both these Farnsworths. Although Selby was twice the size of Harry, they had that same determined look on their faces. There was, perhaps, a little gleam in the young man's eyes—an appeal to Caesar, so to speak.

"Eat your breakfast," she commanded harshly. They both came to the table and dug in without a word being said. Abby had lost her desire for breakfast. She stood watching them for a moment, then turned and started for the door.

"But——" Harry was down out of his chair and following her out into the hall. He was doing his best to keep the tears at bay. Abby was caught by the appeal. She kneeled down in order to be face-to-face with him. The kitchen door had swung shut behind them.

"You're not gonna leave us?"

"I can't. I don't have a boat."

"And if you did have a boat, would you?"

Abby shrugged her shoulders. She honestly did not know the answer.

"My dad, he's a very nice guy."

"Is he really? How many others will be willing to give him their recommendations? Your mother?" Abby couldn't believe that she had said that, but the words were out and hanging there.

"I—I dunno." The boy was biting on his lip. "I don't know nothin' about that. Nobody told me nothin'. But my dad, he's a fine man."

"All right," Abby said softly. "Let's say, just for argument, that you're right. So?"

"So he's trying to do too many things. He works all day and night, and every time he gets some money my mother comes and takes it all away from us."

Take note, Abby told herself. My mother comes and takes it all away from *us*. She could even hear the capital letters in Harry's voice. So that's what drives Selby Farnsworth—alimony?

"Where does your mother live, Harry?"

"We had this house in Palm Beach. After the divorce Mommy got that house, only Dad has to pay all the bills."

"That *is* troublesome," Abby said, sighing. She knew indeed what troubles divorce could bring. Not the least among them was money. And yet, what could *she* do? She barely made enough money doing her book reviews to feed and clothe herself.

"I'm sorry to hear all this," she told the boy. "But there's really nothing I can do about it, is there? Unless you might be able to convince your mother to come back?"

For a moment there was a flash of happiness in the boy's eyes, and then it faded. "You wouldn't believe what a mess they've made of things," he said, in that almost-adult voice of his. "There ain't no way they could come together. No way!"

Abby's knees were aching. So was her heart. She straightened up to her full height, running her fingers through her mass of unruly curls. "I wish there was something I could do to help," she said, "but I can't think of any way I could convince your mother to come back to the family." If I could, would I? she added silently.

"And now I have to get back upstairs. I have a million things left to do, and my vacation time is getting short." She bent over and kissed the top of his head, then turned and headed for the stairs. There was an echo in the big stairwell, but as she mounted the stairs she could not hear what Harry was saying under his breath!

"Maybe a substitute?"

Selby popped out through the kitchen door at just that moment. "What are you two talking about?"

"Cabbages and kings," Abby said, laughing.

"Yeah, that's what we were talking about," Harry agreed.

"Come give me another chance at chess," Selby asked. "One game takes all."

From the second step Abby watched them as they walked, holding hands, down toward the dining room. At the door Selby stopped and looked back at her. "There's a sucker born every minute," he announced dolefully. And then he grinned at her.

Abby settled back on her bed and made a face at the five books lying beside her. All her notes and comments were complete. She needed only to recheck them in the memory of her laptop computer, then feed the whole report back to Washington. The reviews had been difficult. Two of the books were terrible. She had fumbled for hours trying to find something nice to say, without missing the point. She hadn't had much luck. Selby Farnsworth, and that grin of his, was haunting her work. The other three books had been acceptable novels. The reviews had rolled off her fingers at a hundred words a minute.

From downstairs she heard a yip of triumph, and feet running. The front door slammed. Abby pushed her work aside and went over to the window. Harry was out on the sloping grass at the front of the house, playing ball with Cleo—and his father. They're running like young idiots, she told herself. Cleo's out of her class.

And how about you, Selby Farnsworth? You're playing in a fast league yourself. Lots of men your age run straight into heart attacks by doing things like this! Her hands subconsciously moved toward the window. Watch what you're doing, she commanded herself. It's none of your business!

She started checking her computer work at high speed, making corrections as she went. The world seemed to have slowed down for her. All she could hear was the faint sound of the waves on the beach, the occasional sound of the ferries going back and forth from Cape Cod to the islands and the shouts of the Farnsworths as they played ball out on the lawn.

By five o'clock the work was done. She got up for a stretch, then went into the cupboard for her portable telephone. The connection was established quickly. In no more than five minutes her computer terminal was connected into the *Mirror*'s facsimile circuit. She keyed the transmit key on her modem, and watched as a burst of tones carried her stories through the air and down the lines. When it was finished, her machine signaled her, printed out a receipt from the Washington newspaper, and shut itself down. She took another big stretch. The front door slammed down below as the Farnsworths and her dog came tramping in.

Time to get going, she told herself. Woman's work is never done. And then, because *some* of that work was getting to be enjoyable, she went downstairs.

The men were already waiting for her in the kitchen. "Who won the chess game?" she asked as she picked up the fish and set it up on the sideboard.

"Don't ask," Selby grumbled. "I should have played the dog."

"You need to guard your queen," his son teased. "Even Cleo could have beaten you today!"

"Gratitude! Familial respect!" Selby complained. "Shadup!"

Abby did her best to hide her grin as she rubbed salt, pepper and margarine into the fillets. While they squabbled in a friendly fashion she walked over to the refrigerator to see what else might be available. The interior, which had been three-quarters empty yesterday, was packed to its limit. She looked over her shoulder at the two of them.

"Santa Claus has come early?"

"See, Dad," the boy said gloomily. "I told you she was too smart for that."

"Would you believe we dug up all those vegetables down in the garden?"

"I might," Abby returned. "I see also you found a convenient cow passing through, who gave homogenized milk?"

"It does sound a little farfetched. Would you believe I signaled a passing boat yesterday and they delivered a box of stuff?"

"That I could almost believe," Abby said, laughing.

"And he's coming back every day until we leave," Harry contributed.

"In that case, Harry, you can peel the carrots while your father washes off the potatoes."

"Slave labor." They both groaned but set to, while Abby wrapped the fish and the potatoes in aluminum foil. It was so companionable that Selby was whistling and Abby was humming a little tune as the dinner cooked. "Almost like——" And Abby clapped a hand over her mouth. Almost like a real family, she was about to say.

The meal was delicious. At least that was what Harry said. Abby stared at Selby, giving him a moment to contribute, but he had his mouth full, and said not a word.

But a dinner spiced by little Harry's wild imagination could be nothing other than fun. He was a *Star Trek* devotee, and the table became the *Enterprise*. All believable, Abby told herself as it all came to an end in a burst of laughter. From force of habit she moved to the sink with the dishes.

"We'll do the dishes," Selby said as he came over beside her.

"Catch me. I think I'm fainting," Abby returned. "In all the years since I was ten years old I did dishes at home, and none of my brothers ever offered to lift a finger!" She faked a faint, and Selby caught her, sweeping her off her feet. It seemed so easy. She tucked her head in against his shoulder and smiled up at him.

She's a big girl, Selby told himself as he swung her up into his arms. Big and firm—and soft. And she jiggles! It was hard not to grin. He felt like a kid who had inherited a candy store.

"Be careful," his son called. "You might drop her."

"Thanks a lot for your confidence," he replied. He carried her out of the kitchen, across the hall to the dining room, where a fire already blazed in the fireplace. A padded captain's chair stood near the fireplace. He set her down as gently as possible, pulled a footstool under her legs, and leaned over to kiss her forehead.

"What was that for?" she whispered.

"Does it have to be for something?" he asked softly. She nodded. "Then put it down as gratitude for a fine meal," he said. The smile on her face faded. Or put it down to lust, he told himself. Or friendship. Or maybe even—no, that bit about love at first sight is a bunch of baloney. I tried that route once and it didn't work. But wouldn't it be fun to come home to a girl like this? Or is it all just cupboard love?

He added one more kiss. This one on her cheek. If she had given him the slightest sign, he knew, he would have grabbed her, cuddled her against him, run his hands down across those pert breasts, and further. But she made not a wiggle. He forced himself to take his hands off her shoulders. It was difficult.

Back in the kitchen, Harry hadn't stirred a stump. He was still sitting at the table, a big grin on his face. "Hey, kid, what happened with the dishes?"

"I don't think I could reach the sink. Besides, *you* promised, not me."

"You get your little round bottom over here," he said. "You can stand on a chair. I wash, you dry!"

"Slave driver," his son muttered as he dragged a chair over to where the action was.

Across the hall Abby lay back in her chair and rubbed her hands in the warmth of the fireplace. The room wasn't cold; the hand rubbing was just a gesture of contentment. She closed her eyes and let the chatter from the kitchen run by her. Her daydreams flashed by in violent colors. No black and white for her. Selby Farnsworth. A man to be proud of. A man who—was convinced that he needed his former wife back again? The thought brought her little dream to a sudden stop. And just then Harry and his father came over into the dining room and woke her up.

"I don't really know where the time has gone," Selby said as he gave her shoulder a little shake. "Seven o'clock. And Little Boy Blue here is dragging his feet. What's next on the agenda?"

"Bath and bed?" Abby suggested.

"What, again?" Harry protested. "If I keep washing, there'll be nothing left of me. In my school they said that the average guy uses up all his skin every seven years and manufactures new. Mine ain't gonna last half that much. Then what?"

"Don't worry," his father said. "We'll pass a law. Upstairs you go. Bath time. Abby, would you like to participate?"

"Now just a darn minute," the boy protested. "You expect a *girl* to give me a bath? Not on your pea-pickin' life!"

"You didn't object when your mother gave you baths."

"Well, Abby ain't my mother. And I was a lot younger then."

"I wouldn't want to cause a rift in the Farnsworth family," Abby contributed. "I can't say that I'm all that keen about giving him his bath myself. Why don't you two go ahead? I'll meet you when the orgy is over."

"What's that mean—orgy?" the boy questioned as he went upstairs just ahead of his dad. Abby watched. The boy was skipping stairs and laughing. His father was plodding along, one step at a time. She didn't hear the answer, although she strained her ears. It would have been interesting to learn just how Selby defined the word.

Upstairs in the bathroom Selby Farnsworth finally discovered how to turn things on. It was an ornate bathtub, but there were no labels on any of the taps, handles or spouts. So he experimented. He was leaning all the way across the tub when he managed to find the tap for the shower. Little Harry laughed up a storm.

"Hey, kid," he said as he pulled his head back out of the spray, "let's not have any jokes. Remember I'm the big man in this house."

"You may be the big wet man," his son said, giggling, "but you'd better look out because that lady is a *big* girl."

And that's for sure, Selby thought as he fumbled for a towel. A big beautiful girl. Leave it to my son to spot the single important factor in life.

"You like her?" he asked.

"For a girl she's pretty nice," the boy commented. "And you?"

"You're right, Harry. Pretty and nice. For a girl, that is."

"Nicer than that skinny one you used to date?"

"Get in the tub," his father commanded. "Critics I don't need."

Twenty minutes of splashing and laughing and gamesmanship followed. After which he had the boy climb out, dried him off thoroughly, and tucked him into his pyjamas.

"Well, sir," he said to the boy, "how do you like that? A bath every night."

"What?" the boy said indignantly.

"A bath every night," he repeated. "That's the way Ms. Spencer says it has to be. A bath every night. Come on, let's get you to bed."

Harry cocked his head to one side and looked up at his father, who stood twice his height. "You're just doing that to get on her good side," he grumbled. "Why don't we just buy us a dog?"

"Git!" His father took a swing at the little man's bottom, purposely missing.

"I'm going, I'm going," Harry protested, and dashed for his bedroom, laughing. His father stopped long enough to pick up the towels and hang them up, and then followed along down the corridor. Abby was waiting for him at the bedroom door.

"I haven't seen him this happy in years," Selby told her. "It makes my heart feel good."

"I want a bedtime story," Harry called. They both went in, to find the child already under the blankets, with a comforter pulled up to his chin. "I want a bedtime story."

"I don't know any bedtime stories," Selby confessed ruefully. "*Goldilocks*? I can't remember how it ends."

"Not them old stories," Harry protested. "Something new."

Abby sat down on the side of his bed and said, "How about this one? There is a huge statue made out of stone, sitting in the desert of Egypt. It's called the Sphinx. And this is how it got its name. All right?"

"Sounds good," Harry said. "But no smooching. Go ahead."

"Once upon a time, four thousand sixty-three years ago—it was springtime, I think, probably May—a scrawny little rabbit named Peter Popodopolis——"

"A rabbit?" Harry asked incredulously.

"Don't interrupt," Abby said. "I'm telling the story. You just listen."

"So I'm listening," the boy said. He squirmed a little closer to Abby, resting against her arm.

"Not *just* a rabbit," Abby remarked. "The Popodopolis family were famous—not for their good looks, or their charm, but for their survivability. Now, where was I?"

"A scrawny little Peter," Harry prompted. "Way back then——?"

"Okay." Abby moved closer to the boy and dropped one arm over his shoulder. Harry squirmed a tiny bit closer. Over the child's head Abby could see Selby's shadowed face, looking not exactly well pleased at the loss of his son's attention.

"Peter was an orphan and he lived in Memphis, a city in Egypt. As an orphan, he had to earn his own living. So he was apprenticed to a stonecutter, and for two years Peter Popodopolis was kept inside a dirty old tent, cutting stones and squaring corners for the pyramids. He was not very good at it.

"On the final day of his apprenticeship he was hauled up before the master builder, who offered him a diploma in stonecutting, wished him well and directed him to go away.

"'If there is one thing I want to be sure of,' the master builder said to his foreman, 'it's that this new journeyman doesn't ever work for me.'

"So Peter reported in down at the palace, from where most of the work was controlled, and he met the senior officer of the Pharaoh's government. The Pharaoh was, of course you know, the king of Egypt. This official who controlled all the work was called the seneschal. When Peter reported in to him he was told, 'Young man, we don't have anything for you at the moment, but I'll put you on the payroll. Down by the first pyramid we have an extra-big stone that we can't use. That's your stone. You go down there, figure out what to do with it, and sooner or later we will accept from you a proposition and you can cut your own monument as your masterpiece. How does that sound?'

"'That sounds great,' Peter said. 'I'll rush right down.'

"'You'd better get yourself a couple of big chisels,' the seneschal said. 'This is a rough, rough stone.'

"So Peter Popodopolis——" And Abby stopped.

"He's fallen asleep," Selby whispered.

"The poor little tyke has worn himself out," Abby murmured.

"Or that's some magical trait you have, storytelling," Selby said as he followed her out into the hall.

"Yes, it is," Abby grinned up at him. "I've had a lot of practice. I have more nieces and nephews than you can count on your hands and feet."

"Now don't leave me hanging. Whatever happened to the rabbit?"

"For that, sir," Abby said, smiling, "you'll have to wait for another day."

"Why do I have to wait?" he asked as they came to the head of the stairs. He stopped her by the simple expedient of putting a hand on each of her shoulders.

She looked up at him and laughed. "You have to wait because I haven't made up what happens next."

"Oh, brother," he said, and walked down the stairs behind her. Almost by intuition they both turned at the foot of the stairs and went out into the dusk—the quiet, peaceful dusk, with the occasional sound of the steamship whistles as they navigated the narrow channels from Woods Hole. Stars pierced the velvet heaven and all was well with Abby's world.

"Notice the lights," she said. "The fishing fleet making its way into New Bedford harbor. That's a tough way to make a living." She leaned back against him and his arms enfolded her. She had been chilly; in the warmth of his arms things were better. One of his hands ruffled her hair.

"Precious," he murmured.

"My hair?"

"Your everything." His lips touched the nape of her neck, and then he slowly turned her to face him. Again those questing lips—gently, momentarily, like the wing of a butterfly beating against her. They withdrew and returned again, firm, warm, precious, and she succumbed entirely, letting the world riot by itself. When he had finished he leaned back and looked very, very complaisant. "There," he said, "I told you so."

"You told me what?" she asked as her head stopped spinning.

"I told you that—or didn't I tell you? I guess I didn't. Excuse me, I have to do this again." So he gathered her up again in his arms and once more she was elevated from the world, from cares, lost in Xanadu as she floated gently on top of that single kiss.

"Now then," he said finally, "I'm sure I told you."

"I still don't believe that you told me anything," she said, sighing. "Do it again."

He gathered her up again in those strong, warm arms and did just that.

CHAPTER FIVE

ABBY slept in on Sunday until Cleo began to jump madly at the locked door of her bedroom, barking her loudest. Abby groaned, stretched, managed to open one eye and said to her favorite dog, "Shadup."

Cleo came over to the bed, whined and then ran right back to assault the door. Meantime, in back of all of this there was a noise coming from downstairs, a shout of elation—maybe two shouts.

"Oh, Lord," Abby told her dog. "More of this and I'll trade you in for a bowl of goldfish!" Her dog whined at her, and waited by the door.

Abby staggered out of bed, walked over to the door, unlocked it, and opened it just wide enough for Cleo to squeeze her way through. Long after the dog's tail had disappeared down the corridor Abigail, still in a daze, said, "Go," and closed the door again. It hardly seemed worthwhile to go back to bed now. The sun was shining—bright, cold sunshine, the sun of September, the promise of winter—soon. But down below there was still this rage of noise thundering up the stairs at her. She shrugged her shoulders, not hurrying too fast, and stepped out of her nightgown. She chose her usual work clothes—a white blouse, this time with a little ruffle on the collar, and blue jeans.

Downstairs the noise had abated. In fact, it seemed to have torn out of the door and gone down along the back side of the house. Moving cautiously, still not wide awake, Abby fumbled down the stairs.

Selby Farnsworth was standing in the open front door with a huge smile on his face. Cleo was halfway down the side of the hill, looking for Harry. Harry was evidently the leader in all this parade. He was shouting with all his natural talent and running like the very devil down the side of the hill.

"What in God's name is going on?" Abby asked.

"Ah! Queen Cinderella," Selby said. "Nice to have you up."

"Oh, shadup," she said.

"Now, now, Abigail. That's not the way to talk to nice people."

For a minute Abby felt a flush of embarrassment. She looked up at him and gave a little quirky smile and said, "Well, sir, when you're right, you're right. I apologize. Now, may I ask what in the devil is going on?"

"I wish I could tell you exactly," Selby said. "You remember we talked a day or so ago about the treasure your uncle had on the island?"

"Oh, that's a bunch of nonsense," Abby said. "Who in the world told you a stupid thing like that?"

He grinned at her, showing all his teeth. Something like a wolf, she told herself as she moved a step or two away from him.

"Hesselmeyer," he told her. "The guy who runs the boat rental place in Woods Hole."

Abby managed another step backward. Hesselmeyer was big and brawny and dirty, and looked as if he had sailed with Long John Silver. She had been frightened of him since her sixth birthday, when he'd looked a great deal taller and a million times meaner. Her uncle Theodore had denied the treasure story, but what did *he* know?

"Well," Selby said, "look here. Harry was down early for his breakfast and he poked around in that little side desk in the kitchen and he came up with this." He held up in front of her an eight-by-ten-inch piece of crumpled paper, wrinkled with age, dirtied with fingerprints and mud.

Abby put her hands behind her back, not wanting to touch it. "And what in the world is that?"

"It's a map," Selby said. "It's a treasure map—can't you see?"

"All I can see is that it's a map of the island," Abby said. "What more do you want me to see?"

"Looky here," he said. "Here is the doorway that we're standing in."

"In which we're standing," she corrected gently.

He glared down at her. "It's marked D," he said, defying her to say anything. "And then way down here in this corner is a place marked X. X marks the spot. That's where the treasure must be."

"You've got to be joking!" Abby said. "I think I'll go have some breakfast."

"Well, I've got to go help Harry," he said. "Do you mind if we hunt for treasure on your island?"

"Lord no," Abby said. "Hunt away. Everything on this island is mine. And everything you find we share. How's that?"

"I'm flabbergasted," he commented. "You are certainly some changeable lady." He turned around and started off along the corner of the house after the dog and the boy.

"Oh, well," Abby said aloud as she watched him walk away. "All this time I had him pegged as God's gift to the devil and yet every time I see him he seems more and more—well, look at that." Far down at the corner of the island, just at the edge of her available line of sight, Harry had stopped, confused, and his father had caught up with him. The man put his arm around the boy, comforting. It was a small move, but a very companionable sight.

There's something more to Selby Farnsworth than I've ever thought, Abby mused. Something very nice. Isn't that a surprise? Instead of going off to the kitchen as she had previously said she would, she went out. She closed the door behind her and walked down to where the others were waiting.

"I think it's right here," Harry said excitedly. "Look, there's that shed and directly south of it is that tree, and the X on the map is right square in between 'em."

"You could be right," his father said in his slow drawl. "Of course, there aren't many treasures left in the world, you know. I don't know of any pirate treasures left in this area, but if you'd like to dig, then dig away."

"I'll have to find the shovel," the boy said.

"With your fishing gear," Abby called. "You remember you left them all together?" Harry nodded and was gone before she could add another word. She folded her arms across her breasts and looked up at Selby. "You know this is a wild-goose chase. Don't you?" she said.

"What difference does it make?" he returned. "The boy wants to do something. He's excited about it. And I'm going to help him. That's what fathers are for."

"You're a better man than I thought, Gunga Din," Abby said.

He looked back at her and chuckled. "Gunga Din? Huh!"

"Well, good luck to you."

To her surprise he added, "That's a lovely blouse you have on." In all of the time they had been together, he had never uttered a kind word about her appearance.

"Well, thank you," she returned. If he had been offering her a coin she would have bitten it to see if it were real or fake. She felt the same skepticism about his compliment. But two could play at the compliment game. "That's a very nice shirt you're wearing."

"Oh, come off it, Abby," he chided. "This is the same shirt I've worn for the last five days. Somehow or other I've got to get to a washing machine. Are you going to stay and help us excavate?"

"No, I think not. I think I'll take a stroll along the pier and then go back up for breakfast. Have you both eaten?"

"No, we haven't. The excitement's too high," Selby said.

"When I get back, I'll see if I can't whip up something," Abby promised. She watched for a moment as the man and the boy joined together. One large shovel, one small shovel. They had come to "X"; you could see it plainly in their faces.

Abby chuckled to herself and walked away slowly. This was more like living. This was more like it was when she and her brothers were still living at home—before *they* all grew up and got married and left her behind. Maybe some day I'll meet the right man and I'll get married, she thought. She wasn't quite sure of that. Her brothers all made sloppy husbands. Was Selby Farnsworth any better?

She whistled for her dog. Cleo, tired of the maneuvers with the shovels, came running after her. "We're going for a walk, dog," she said. Cleo barked. "Walk" wasn't one of her favorite words. Mind you, she would put up with it for a time, but it wasn't a favorite like "lunch" or "dinner." But she followed Abby as she wound slowly down around the little hill. Down to the sandy beach she strolled, to where the flagpole and the saluting gun stood, wrapped in silence. Things were not as they used to be. Abby took a good look around. She well remembered the saluting gun. Her great-uncle had been a veteran of World War I and when he had been in residence on his island he had run up the flag every day and saluted it with a single round from his cannon.

She looked up at the flagpole. It looked as if the ropes were all entangled—too much so for use, but the possibility was there. What I've got to do is to get some brave soul to shimmy up the pole and get the lines untangled, she thought. Some brave—some brave Selby Farnsworth? It was hard to repress the giggle.

She turned around and looked out to sea. Directly in front of her was the narrow passage that led from Woods Hole out to Martha's Vineyard. Coming through that channel toward her island was a fairly large cabin cruiser. It was flying the American flag and making an approach as if it meant to land on her island. Of course, "land" was a euphemistic term. Very few boats could actually "land" on her island. Dinghies, rowboats, that sort of craft could approach to the end of the pier. There was hardly enough sand around the pier to make for a beach landing.

This cruiser pulled up, perhaps forty or fifty feet offshore, dropped an anchor and then swung around into the current. At the stern someone was lowering a small rowboat. A man was at the oars as it came around the bow of the cruiser and began to work its way toward the island—a man who was obviously not too familiar with rowing and rowboats. He was "catching more crabs than water," as the local folk would say. Abby studied his style. It was always pleasant to see someone who rowed worse than she did. He came up to the end of the pier where there was a little mooring hook, tied up his little boat, and then looked up at her.

The tide was in and so his head and shoulders were even with the top of the pier. "Hello there," he called in a cheerful voice. He was a little man with very round,

round cheeks, a little hair on top of his head, a great deal of hair on his chin.

"Hello yourself," she called out. "You lost or something?"

"Oh, no," he said. "I want to tie up and visit for a spell."

"I don't think we can allow that," she called back to him. "This is a private island. We don't allow visitors without prior approval."

"But that can't possibly mean me," he said. "I'm from the *Providence Gazette*."

"Oh, I suppose that's nice," Abby said. "I don't read the *Gazette*, but I've heard a great many nice things said about it."

"Well, what I'd like to find out," he said, "is how Congressman Farnsworth is doing."

Abby nibbled on her lower lip for a minute. And then her brain imploded. Book reviewers hardly ever dabbled their toes in the congressional currents, but even non-politicians like Abby Spencer knew that this was the year for barbecuing congressmen. For many a year the private lives of officeholders had been their own to flaunt or conceal. But this year *morality* had raced across the Washington scene. With the year only half over, already two congressmen and one long-term senator had been pilloried by the media, and had lost all their usefulness in office. *Congressman* Farnsworth was a target of considerable more importance than novelist Farnsworth, or lawyer Farnsworth.

The other shoe dropped. Very suddenly Abby Spencer realized that she would not ever willingly do harm to Selby Farnsworth. How could she, when he was the man she loved? He might lie and cheat and steal—like any congressman—but she loved him all the same!

She shook her head negatively. "Congressman Farnsworth? I don't believe I know anybody by that name," she said.

"Oh, come on," the man retorted. "We all know that he's here. You're here. The boy's here. Obviously the congressman is here as well." While Abby was thinking of a suitable reply the reporter climbed up onto the dock.

"I'm afraid you're making a terrible mistake," Abby said. "I'm here because I own this island and I suppose that Congressman Farnsworth is in Washington D.C. Have you checked there?"

"No, but I'm going to check right here," he said. "I'm sure——"

"If I were you," Abby interrupted, "I wouldn't do that. This is a private island."

"You won't hardly lose anything by my finding out where the congressman is," he said. "Everything Farnsworth does is news. The story would be worth fifty dollars. Are you his latest ladybird?" He started to walk toward her.

Abby backed up a step or two. She wasn't exactly sure, but somehow she thought he might have just insulted her. And, moving down the dock in her direction, he looked a little threatening. Another step backward, and she ran right into the muzzle of the saluting cannon. It wasn't really a major weapon, but it did make a loud noise. She took a deep breath to steady her nerves.

"I think," she said, "you'd best not take another step because I don't like to have visitors here. And what I don't like my dog doesn't like and my cannon doesn't like! Cleo, sic 'em."

Her dog looked up at her as if she thought her mistress had finally blown her cool. "Sic 'em" was not a term that had been used since Cleo was a pup. Nonetheless, she was willing to offer some small bit of cooperation. She bellied down to the top of the pier and then gradually worked her way toward the reporter, offering two or three *very* large barks as samples. The reporter took a deep breath and stopped.

He has more guts than I have, Abby told herself. If I didn't know that Cleo was a beggar rather than a biter I'd be running myself! He's not stopping! Find some other persuasion! Her hand caressed the barrel of the cannon. She fumbled behind her and reached into the little tin shed where the blank cartridges were stored.

"If you don't get off my pier——" she threatened. "Are you listening to me? If you don't get off my pier, I'm going to do something very drastic."

"Oh, come on, lady," he said nervously. "What more can you do that's so drastic? Call the dog off, will you?"

"No, I don't think I could call the dog off," she said. "In fact, if you don't get out of here I'm going to fire my cannon at your yacht out there and blow the thing out of the water."

"Hey, lady," he said, aggravated out of his command of the language, "this ain't no pirate's nest. Come on now, what the devil are you doing?"

Abby pulled the lever that unlocked the breech of her cannon, shoved in the paper cartridge load, closed it and then, just for effect, reached down and picked up one of the six-inch iron balls that were stacked beside the cannon to give it the impression of being a real weapon. The ball clattered down the barrel. She carefully cranked the muzzle of the cannon up so that the ball would not roll out and spoil the illusion.

"Hey, lady, watch it," he said nervously.

Abby reached for the lanyard. "Now I told you. If you don't get off my island I'm going to blow your boat out of the water."

"Lady, you've got to be crazy," he said. "What do you think this is?"

"I think this is Umatec Island and if you're not off it by the time I count ten," she said, "I'm going to give you a demonstration of *The Camp Fire Girls* and *The Pirates of Penzance* all at once."

"Lady, lady," he said, coaxing, "come on now." He took a step forward. Cleo growled. The reporter stopped.

"Three, four, five," Abby counted.

The man took another half step backward, Cleo barked one more time. The dog was beginning to enjoy herself. From the yacht offshore there came a hail as if someone was using a bullhorn.

"Nine, ten," Abby said.

The man looked at her, aghast, as her right hand pulled hard on the lanyard. There was never any instant reaction with a cannon of this type. There was a deadly moment or two of silence before the cartridge caught fire. It went off with a loud, loud noise that sent the sea gulls squawking into the air. A puff of smoke flared out of the muzzle followed by a flash as the remainder of the paper cartridge was ejected. Abby was more impressed than the sea gulls. Her great-uncle had never let her stand this close when the gun was being fired. Even Cleo was startled.

But that was only part of the excitement. The old ratchet that controlled the elevation of the barrel was jarred out of its lock by the force of the explosion. The barrel, which had formerly been pointed toward the sky, gradually turned downward until it slammed into its stops, with the muzzle almost dragging on the ground.

The reporter stood frozen in position. Abby, with both hands to her ears, closed her eyes. Cleo gave a weak whine, tucked her tail in, and ran to get behind her mistress. Out of the barrel rolled the six-inch cannonball.

It seemed as if the whole world had stopped to see what was going on. The ball was not making any great speed at all, but it thumped down onto the old planks of the pier and started rolling slowly.

"Holy hell," the reporter yelled as he backed to the end of the pier. The cannonball rolled steadily down the length of the dock, came to the far end, seemed to hesitate a moment, and then plunged over the edge.

The man backed up a little bit and looked over. "Oh, my God, look what you've done to my boat," he cried.

"What have I done?" Abby asked.

"What have you done? You've shot a hole in my boat!" he roared.

"Can you—swim?" Abby asked. In the moment between the "you" and the "swim" her opponent had given a desperate yell and dived into the water. "I guess you can," Abby called after him, but by that time he was already twenty feet away, doing the Brooklyn version of the Australian crawl.

Another thought struck her mind—Good Lord, they're looking for Selby! He must have heard the shot, and if he comes down to the beach they'll see him from the yacht, and—— With that thought in mind, Abby turned and ran for her life around the corner of the hill.

Selby and Harry both stopped digging when they heard the cannon go off.

"What on earth is that?" Selby asked.

"That's Abby's cannon," his son informed him. "You didn't know she had a cannon, did you? Oh, she's got everything!"

"A cannon? Come on, boy." Selby drove his shovel deep into the earth and started running. Harry, not willing to be left too far behind, did exactly the same. The two of them whistled down around the base of the hill, but, before they could come out into the open on the beach, here came Abby. She was running like the wind; in fact, she was running so fast, so furiously, so undirected that she smashed her head right into Selby's stomach and he sat down with a terrific, "Uhh!"—just like an accountant meeting one of the professional New York Giants head to head on the playing field some Sunday. It took him the better part of a minute to get some of his breath back.

"What?" he managed to gasp, and it was just barely a gasp.

She looked at him, almost with tears in her eyes. "They're going to get you," she said, and started to cry. "And it's all my fault!"

He took another deep breath, and two more. "What in the world are you saying?" he asked. He was sprawled out flat on his back. She was squirming on top of him with her head on his shoulder, trying to get closer. The soft warmth of her swirling hair swept over his face. He gloried in it. Somehow this woman had more effect on him than all the women he had ever known. He tried to sit up to kiss her ear and then she recovered. She sat up in his lap.

"I—uh—there was this reporter," she said. "He was looking for Congressman Farnsworth. Do you know who that is?"

"Of course I know who that is. That's me. And what were they looking for me for?"

"Well, I don't know," Abby said haughtily. "I'm not much up with representatives and high-class lawyers. But he looked to be very, very eager to find out where Representative Farnsworth is. Why didn't you tell me?"

"Why didn't I tell you what?"

"Why didn't you tell me you were a politician?"

"Because I didn't want you to know. Because I thought surely you'd be angry. So what happened? Did you shoot him down with your cannon?"

"I didn't shoot him down with my cannon. I sounded off my saluting cannon and just by the absolute, the veriest impossible, unbelievable circumstance the cannonball fell out of the front end of the gun and rolled down the dock and——"

"Geez, I missed all the fun," Harry said. "Will you fire it again?"

"Did you sink his boat? Abby, do we have to go rescue him?"

"No need for that. He's swimming back. It's only fifty or sixty feet back to the yacht anchorage, so he'll be all right. But this is only one fellow. Now suppose we all three sit carefully together and you explain to me why reporters from the Providence newspapers are trying to invade my island looking for some representative?" And with that she moved to an adjacent rock and glared at him with fire sparking out of her green gold eyes.

Harry could see that there were storms brewing between his father and Abby so he very quietly started back to the treasure dig. They could fight without him. People fighting brought back memories he didn't like. To his great relief, Cleo decided to go with him.

"Well," Selby said, "it's like this." And before he said another word he stopped to think. What would it be like if I tell her that I'm an elected representative from Ohio? And suppose in another three or four hours there is another, bigger invasion from the sea and more reporters—everybody looking for Congressman Farnsworth? What then? Well, of course, here's Congressman Farnsworth camped out on a deserted island in the middle of Narragansett Bay with his son and this *very* significant other. Who is not, by the way, his wife.

"Abby," he said, trying to look very, very calm, "would I lie to you?"

She smiled a little bit, just a little curve to the tip of her lips. "Have you ever done anything else?" she asked.

"Perhaps we haven't necessarily used the truth to its fullest extent," he said cautiously.

"Hurrah for that," Abby said. "I'm happy to hear. Would you care to expand on that?"

"Well," he said, "my father always used to tell me that 'the truth was a pearl of great price.' " And then he stopped.

"And what else did your father tell you?" Abby prodded him.

"It's simple," he said. "You don't use a pearl of great price every day out in the open. You use it carefully. You keep it stored away."

Oh, brother, Abby thought. Talk about logic! "Is that how you got to be elected congressman?"

"Well, perhaps it had something to do with it," he said. "Yes, that's how I got elected. Now, are you going to call the newspapermen and tell them the whole story?"

"Of course not," she said. "That would be a silly thing to do. So you didn't tell me because you thought I couldn't handle it?"

"Something like that. Why are you shaking?"

"I can't handle it," she muttered, and hesitated, unable to reach a decision.

"Come on. Let's show you what it is that Harry dug up in his treasure hunt." He jumped to his feet, extended both hands to her and very gently towed her up to her own feet, and then, following the boy, they walked together toward the excavation. His arm was around her waist and her head was comfortably close. He could feel her heartbeat as it slowed to a gentler rhythm. It was a wonderful feeling.

"Well, now," Harry said when they got up to the site. "You can see where we've been digging. We've found——"

"Two tin cans," his father interrupted. "Two tin cans, a few bones, a little bunch of paper, and an old bottle. Now what do you suppose that means?"

"I can't say," Abby said. "This is the place that was marked on the map?"

Harry whipped the map out of his pocket, spread it out carefully in front of her and pointed out the X mark and the house.

After close perusal, Abby said, "Oh! I know what this is."

"What is it?" Harry asked excitedly.

"I'm sorry to tell you, Harry," she said. "You have rediscovered my great-uncle's garbage pit. It got so full about ten years ago that he decided to cover it over, mark it, and start another one down closer to the other end of the island. What you have is the kitchen midden, and since that's what all good archaeologists wind up with eventually maybe you ought to get your father to explain something about this to you."

"Oh, hell," Selby said. "A kitchen midden."

"What was that you said?" Harry asked, puzzled.

"A garbage pit," Abby repeated. "Now come on, you guys—let's go on up to the house and get yourselves washed up. I'm going to cook a lunch for you that you'll never believe."

"I don't know if I'd want a lunch I couldn't believe," Harry said.

"Shadup," his father said as he pulled the visor of his son's baseball cap down over his eyes and grabbed his hand.

* * *

At about eight o'clock that night Selby sent his son off to bed. The boy came by the kitchen where Abby was looking over the rest of the stores. He poked his head in and said, "Can I hear the rest of that rabbit story?"

"Well, I don't see why not," Abby said. "You get yourself upstairs, scrub your hands and face again——"

"I already did that four times today," Harry objected. "I could wear my skin away."

"You'll do a thousand times more within ten years," Abby said very solemnly. "Scoot you go, boy." She put down her tea towel and looked at the mass of dirty dishes. "'Never do today what you can put off until tomorrow,'" she told herself, sighing. Harry made a dash for the stairs. Abby followed more slowly. Selby was rattling the door of the locked room next to the kitchen.

"How about this room, Abby?" he said. "I haven't been into it. Have you?" It was the room between the kitchen and the bathroom.

"No, I haven't been in it," Abby said. "At least, not to my best remembrances. Shall we give it a try?"

"I would," Selby said, "but it's locked. I don't know of any other door that's locked in the house. Why this one?"

"Well, I don't know that either," Abby confessed. "Maybe it was the one room that my uncle Theo wanted to keep just for himself. You know he was not a person to be very friendly with others. He liked to be the leader. He liked to have his own way about things and he liked to keep people out of his study. This might be it. I tell you what—all the keys to the house are hanging on a hook in the dining room. Can you get them?"

He was back again within seconds, with that big, boyish grin on his face. It was enough to give her heart a little twist. "There. Now, then."

"Give them each a try," Abby suggested. "I don't know which one fits what."

For fifteen minutes they stood there trying keys until there was a yell from the top of the stairs. "Hey," Harry yelled. "What about my bedtime story?"

"Coming," Abby promised. "Coming." And at that moment Selby found the key that opened the door. It squeaked as they pushed. The flashlight that Selby carried gave a tiny beam of light. He swung it around the room. It was undoubtedly the center of Uncle Theodore's domain, a quiet refuge. The study was filled with books, rack upon rack all around the sides. A huge desk squatted in the middle of the windowless room. A very comfortable old chair squeaked when she sat in it to try it out. There were a few filing cabinets set in the corners.

"The study," she said. "Now, if I were to think of all the possible things that my uncle Theo would want to store away for himself, this would be the place where they'd be located."

"Why don't we look it over?" Selby suggested. "It wouldn't take too much time."

"You don't mean to tell me that you're still eager, after digging all morning in the kitchen midden?" Abby asked.

"Oh, I'm not tired." There was a dull clank. "I've been carrying Harry's prizes around," he said. "I suppose I could just leave them here?" The beam of the flashlight momentarily illuminated the top of the desk—and the cans and the bottle rescued from the garbage pit.

"I promised a little boy the end of a bedtime story. Are you going to search or are you going to come with me?"

"That's a Hobson's choice," he grumbled. "One or the other, but never both?"

"But never both," Abby agreed as she fumbled for the door.

"All right." She could hear the sigh of regret in his voice as he said it. "Let's go upstairs and get the little boy settled. And then we'll——"

"And then we'll have a good night's sleep," Abby interrupted. "'Sufficient unto the day is the evil thereof.'" With that, she walked out.

"Nothing I hate worse than people who quote from the Bible," Selby said as he trailed after her down the corridor. "It shows up my ignorance."

The boy was already in bed, suspiciously in bed, lying straight out beneath the covers as no little boy ever did when he was sleeping.

"You're asleep?" Abby asked.

"No," Harry said, "I'm not asleep. I'm just resting my eyes."

"Is that a fact? Why is the bottom of your bed wiggling so, young man?"

"Wiggling?" Harry said innocently. "I have no idea!"

"Is that a fact?" said Abby. "Cleo, get out of there."

There was a little rustle among the covers, the dog barked once or twice and found her way out of the sheets.

"Now," Abby said as she leaned closer to the bed, "here we go to finish our story about Peter Popodopolis, and how the Sphinx got its name. You remember Peter?"

"Peter the rabbit. Yeah, I remember. What happened next?"

"Well, if you remember, Peter Popodopolis had just graduated from stone-cutters school and had been assigned a very, very large stone for his very own work down on the beach between the river and the Great Pyramid of Pharaoh Hohumhotep."

"Hoho...who?"

"I beg your pardon—that was Hohumhotep. Yes, he was one of the great pharaohs. So one fine day Peter was standing by his rock and along came the Pharaoh with all his dignitaries and all his horses and his hunting dogs—the whole paraphernalia. Himself pulled up in front of Peter and he said, 'Well?'

"And Peter said, 'Yes, Your Majesty.'

"And His Majesty said, 'What is it that you are going to do with this great big rock?'

"Peter gave him his biggest and best smile, because he didn't know what he was going to do with the rock. 'Well, Majesty,' he said, 'I'm going to carve here some great memorial to the greatest person in the kingdom.'

"'Ah,' Hohumhotep said, 'a little more imagination, a great magnificent—how about you should carve my head, right here? Would that be something?'

"'Yes sir, that would be something,' Peter said. He didn't really know *what* it would be, because he had never really carved a head before. If you remember, all he had ever done was to square off the corners of the blocks of stone due to be used in the Great Pyramid—and he wasn't that good even at doing that!

"'Okay,' Hohumhotep said, 'two weeks I'll give you.'

"'Two weeks?'

"'Two weeks,' Pharaoh said. 'Seneschal, write that down.' Behind him in his big chariot the seneschal reached for a fresh roll of papyrus and wrote the instructions. With that the Great Pharaoh rode away.

"Peter sat down to ponder all this. Carve a head of the Pharaoh in two weeks? He was really in a lot of trouble, but just about then along came a runner.

"Peter didn't know who it was until this runner got close. It was, in fact, the Pharaoh's wife, and she was running for exercise because she had a tendency to go fat. She stopped in front of Peter and his big rock and said, 'Oh, magnificent. What you ought to do with that is to carve the body of a lion here, which is my tribal insignia.'

"Now this was hard for Peter to understand because the Great Queen had a lisp, a fat tummy, and a vile temper. While Peter was struggling for words, one of the Queen's slaves stumbled in the sand and dropped the majestic parasol. 'Off with his head,' the Queen said. And the order was executed before the Queen had taken two steps.

"Nevertheless, one hardly stands in the middle of the desert in front of the Great Queen and says, 'What did you say, lady?' So he bowed down ceremoniously and said, 'All you have spoken, mighty lady, I shall do.'

"'Two weeks,' the Queen's senior lady-in-waiting said. 'Or else.'

"And with that the Queen went jogging off, leaving Peter faced with a terrible problem. He had to produce two different statues out of one piece of stone. So he got himself a *big* canvas to cover the entire affair and off he went, chip, chip, chip, carving first a little bit of the head in the front, and then after a while, when he got too nervous, carving away at the lion's back end at the other end of the rock.

"Finally, the two-week period was up. Peter had finished. He wasn't quite sure what he had finished because he had never had the time to look at the whole thing together, but he was finished. Along came Pharaoh with his drums, his bugles, and all his of his paraphernalia of office.

"'Aha,' said Pharaoh. 'Is it that you have now concocted a great statue of Hohumhotep the Great?'

"'You'd better believe it, Majesty,' Peter said. 'And it is for looking that I have built this big grandstand

BEFORE MAILING DID YOU...

1. Play your Win-A-Fortune tickets? Don't forget to fill in your name and address in the space provided on the back of your game piece!

2. Play your Lucky 7 Slot Machine game for free books? If you have played your Slot Machine game, you may also play your Ace of Hearts game for a free gift.

Harlequin Reader Service®

Dear Reader,

Get out a coin—kiss it for good luck—and go to work on the WIN-A-FORTUNE tickets enclosed. You could end up a <u>million</u> <u>dollars</u> richer!

By returning these tickets you'll also be in the running for hundreds of other cash prizes we'll be giving away. It costs nothing to play this game—there's no fee, and no purchase is necessary!

We're holding this sweepstakes to introduce you to the benefits of the Harlequin Reader Service®. Scratch off the gold boxes on the enclosed Lucky 7 Slot Machine Game and we'll send you <u>free</u> <u>books</u>!

How many FREE BOOKS will you get? Play the Slot Machine Game and see! These books are absolutely free, with no obligation to buy anything!

The Harlequin Reader Service is **not** like some book clubs. We charge you nothing—ZERO—for your first shipment. And you don't have to make any minimum number of purchases—not even one!

over, please

FOLD ALONG DOTTED LINE AND DETACH CAREFULLY

HOW MANY
FREE BOOKS
ARE YOU ELIGIBLE FOR?
Follow directions below to find out!

With a coin, carefully scratch off the three gold boxes. Then check the chart below to learn how many FREE BOOKS will be yours!

"WIN
FORT

1
If o
and
rev
Gra

2
ly fr
Rea

3

4

Na

Ac

Ci

To
bo
m
3"
60
nu
of
of
FR
no

7 **7** **7**			WORTH FOUR FREE BOOKS!
🔔 🔔 **BAR**			WORTH THREE FREE BOOKS!
🍒 🍒 **BAR**			WORTH TWO FREE BOOKS!
BAR **BAR** **BAR**			WORTH ONE FREE BOOK!

You'll receive brand-new Harlequin Presents® novels. When you scratch off the gold boxes and return this card in the reply envelope provided, we'll send you the books you qualify for <u>absolutely free</u>.

where you and your nobles can watch while I unveil this statue.'

" 'Very considerate of you,' said Hohumhotep, and he started to climb up on to the grandstand. However, one of his servants, who was supposed to catch his cloak when the Pharaoh climbed out of his chariot, missed it, and in consequence the Pharaoh was forced to stop for a moment and say, 'Off with his head.' And then he quietly moved up into the grandstand.

"Peter Popodopolis swallowed hard. 'Off with his head? Good Lord!'

"At just about that minute, here came Her Majesty, riding on the back of an elephant. Well, it was a small elephant, you understand. A nineteen-dollar ninety-five elephant from the shoemakers' guild and restaurant. At any rate, she came up in front of the whole crowd and she said, 'Have you finished my statue?'

"And Peter Popodopolis, not knowing what else to say, bowed his head fully and said, 'Yea, oh, beauteous Majesty, I have finished your statue.'

"He tried to imitate her majestic lisp. The Queen looked at him sternly. 'Are you mocking me, sculptor?' she said.

" 'Not me! Oh, no, not me. I wouldn't dream of it!' Peter said. 'I have this block in my tongue. I can't thay thome wordths.'

" 'Well, lucky for you, I believe it today,' the Queen said. 'Tomorrow I wouldn't. Now get on with it!'

"So the Queen got off her elephant and climbed toward where the Pharaoh was sitting. Now you have to understand, Pharaoh and his Queen hadn't been friendly for the last fifteen years. There were very few things that they did together, except fight. And so they sat glowering at each other while Peter ran around the statue collecting the folds and corners of the canvas cover. He stopped for a moment of prayer, and then pulled it off!

"'My God,' said the Pharaoh, 'look at that. Me, my great lovable face on the body of a lion. Oho! Grand.'

"And the Queen looked at it and said, 'Ugh, awful, awful. What are you doing, sculptor? Did I not tell you to make a lion insignia? What have you done?'

"'Well, I made a very pretty head,' Peter said as he gradually sidled down toward the tunnel which led from the desert to the river. 'What do you think of it?'

"'I'll tell you,' the Queen screamed and she swelled up with pride and glory and bad breath. 'It sphinx!'

"'It really does,' the Pharaoh agreed, and almost fell over laughing. Of course that was a family joke, because the Pharaoh's head preceded the Queen's lion. The clan insignia of the Queen was on the behind, so to speak.

"The queen rose and yelled, 'Off with his head!' and the Pharaoh rose and yelled,

"'Only *I* get to say, Off with his head. Off with his head!'

"At which point the Queen hit the Pharaoh with her parasol, the grandstand collapsed with a terrible crash, and the Queen's elephant trampled everybody and everything in sight.

"Except, that is, for Peter Popodopolis. You will remember that I said in the beginning that the Popodopolis family had one great trait—survivability. So while the royal court was trying to dig itself out Peter sneaked down to the river and stole a reed canoe, and paddled like mad in a northerly direction. He was last seen turning west just outside the great light house at Pharos—but that, of course, is another story.

"And to this day that strange statue towers over the sand, half-lion, half-pharaoh, and everybody calls it the Sphinx.''

In the moment of silence that followed, Abby and Selby both looked down. The little boy had a big smile on his face and he was fast asleep, with Cleo cuddled up beside him.

"Good Lord," Selby whispered. "You've got some nerve. What an awful story."

"I didn't see you rush forward to fill in the gaps," Abby said, "and I thought it was pretty great. It's a true story, you can tell. Just you look on any map and you can see that the Sphinx is still standing there."

"Good Lord," Selby said, "that sphinx!"

It must be true, Abby told herself as she looked over to the man standing beside her. It was a terrible story, but look what it got me. She was standing with her weight on one foot. Selby was standing next to her with his arm around her waist, holding her tightly up against him. And it felt marvelous!

Selby looked down at her and read the message in her eyes. He leaned over and kissed her gently. "That was a good story," he said. "I correct myself. If I were King Hohumhotep—where did you get that name, by the way? Hohumhotep?"

"I got that directly from the king's list. Have you never read the kings list at Memphis?"

"No," Selby said, smiling at Abby. "I haven't hardly been to Memphis since they gave up jazz."

"In Egypt," she spat. "Memphis, Egypt. Idiot——" She was about to say something else when he kissed her again and changed her mind.

CHAPTER SIX

SEPTEMBER was an in-between time in New England. The summer days of August, hot, humid and fit for beach use, had all passed. The colorful days of October had yet to come, when the leaves began to turn crimson and yellow and orange, and people went out driving, to follow the color.

Right after the Labor Day holiday even nature paid attention to the calendar. Little storms popped up here and there, spreading dampness, cold and fog—not the cold of winter but a chill for those who had had a long summer outdoors.

Along with all of this came an occasional major storm. New England, of late, had been the aiming point for a number of hurricanes. Sometimes, in between hurricanes, came line storms, harbingers of the winter to come, and as capable of doing as much damage as any hurricane. It was these line storms that forced people indoors and into a brooding mood.

Monday was one of those days on Umatec Island. Just at noon Abby was sitting in the window seat in her bedroom looking out at the dull rage of wind that swept across the island, the waves that peaked white out in the shallow narrows. Even the birds had taken shelter. They could find no roosts on the island, but over on the mainland, on the flat-roofed malls of Woods Hole and Hyannis, they congregated in their thousands, leaving the storms to the shore and whoever had an adventurous soul.

Abby had some thinking to do. The few days that she had spent on the island with Selby Farnsworth and his son Harry had passed at high speed. She had been caught up with them and fluttered around like a loose leaf in the wind, and now it was time to think.

Selby Farnsworth; what was he? Well, throughout all these days she had finally discovered that he was a congressman from Ohio, that he was a lawyer, and that he was a novelist. But each one of these separate little items did not make a whole. It was like pulling nails to get him to admit who and what he really was. And although she couldn't say *definitely*, it was probable that he was high up on the Baron Munchausen trophy list. He certainly had a wonderful disdain for the truth. What was it that he said? "The truth is a pearl of great price" and should be used "carefully." Oh, Lord, *carefully*, she thought.

But then why am I concerned? He is only a man who's passing through. In a few days—and not many more— we'll both be gone. I'll be back to a desk at the *Mirror*, he'll be writing novels, passing laws and whatever else that congressmen do. That is, whatever congressmen do that is legal and aboveboard.

There was something that bothered her about all of this. When she closed her eyes and thought about Selby Farnsworth, she found that she was not thinking about his jobs and offices. She was thinking about the whole man. The length and breadth of him; the span of his personality. And her thoughts were bothering her. She might call up that smile of his when he told her a real whopper, but her heart would discard that picture and substitute the warmth of his arm around her. She might struggle to bring up his casual methods of raising the boy, and instead there would appear the honey taste of his kisses.

So after struggling for some time Abby gave up. There was not much else to do in the house when rain conspired and boys perspired. Downstairs she could hear the racket as Harry and his father raced through the multiple rooms of the old house doing some sort of indoor game that only males could comprehend. And then things fell silent. Wishing that she could and hoping that she wouldn't, Abby dressed, and walked over to her laptop word processor. A tap of the keys showed that all her assignments were finished and had been transmitted. So there. She could relax perhaps for a day or three and then go home, back to the misery of living in Washington D.C. That was another town she knew about. It was a great place for a few people, but for many, many thousands it was the pits.

Trying to cheer herself up, she dug out a clean blouse, found her best jeans, dressed carefully, brushed her hair until it shone and then started for the stairs. She had no more than stepped out of her room when there was a patter of clawed feet down the hall and Cleo, who had evidently been hiding from the downstairs roughhousing, came clattering up to her, sniffed at her, whined a couple of times and guided her down the stairs. It was a pleasant thing to have a dog big enough to pat without having to bend over. A dog big enough to protect one, a dog full of love and spirit. Cleo stopped long enough to lick her hand.

Downstairs everything was quiet, surprisingly quiet. There was a splatter of childish chatter on occasion and a deep response from Selby, all coming from the dining room. She walked slowly down the hall, and peeked around the wide-open double door. The Farnsworths were crouched, the pair of them, over a chessboard. Little Harry with his intense eyes and his tongue half protruding from his mouth as he leaned forward on his elbows; Selby, equally intent, but not conspicuously so. She could feel what she had denied before. There was between these two males a great love, a great affection, and anybody could feel it. She watched as they played for a moment or two and all she could think of was, His wife gave up all this? I wonder how she could. Rather than disturb them, she idled her way back up the corridor. She checked the door of the study, into which they had practically forced their way the night before. There was not a speck of light inside, it being a windowless room, but there were two or three lamps available. She had got into the practice of carrying matches with her everywhere she went. She lit two of the lamps to brighten up the place. It was a really magnificent little room.

It needed dusting. Abby ran her finger over the hard backs of some of the books on the lower shelves and there was enough dust accumulated there to blacken her finger. But there were varieties of books, some of them dating all the way back to the 1870s. It was hard to believe that her great-uncle would have read such books. Although he had lived through the 1890s, he had only been a boy. It was disturbing to her, because this too was a secret about a man that she thought she had known but obviously hadn't. In all the years she had known her great-uncle she could never remember him sitting down to read. Yet the study was lined from floor to ceiling with books.

On his big desk, which stood in the middle of the room, she could see the prizes that Selby and Harry had dug out of the kitchen midden. Two old beaten-up cans. The Lord only knew what they might have contained. An old wine bottle. Not being an expert in wines, Abby looked at it for a moment, brushed a little bit of the dust off the label, studied it casually and then put it down. The portion of the label she uncovered was in

French, a language far beyond her ken. But she did know that French wine was famous—and could be expensive. She shrugged her shoulders and sat the bottle down in the center of the desk, and flanked it by the two cans.

There was a little breaking-up noise from across the hallway in the dining room. Abby sat down in the big chair in the study and whirled herself around in half circles. The chair was just her size; her feet reached the floor. Although the springs squeaked from time to time it was a comfortable chair. She leaned back and at that moment Selby, who was passing by, looked in.

"Ah, this is where you're hiding."

She looked up at him. He was a man. Good or bad? Hero or villain? Good Lord, she still didn't know. "I wasn't hiding," she said softly. "I was contemplating."

"Ah, meditating?"

"I guess you could say that. I was doing that too."

"What were you meditating on?"

"If it wouldn't cause your ego to be too inflated," she said, "I was meditating on you."

"Well," he said. He came into the room and closed the door after him. "This deserves more investigation. What thoughts came to your mind?" He walked around the desk and turned her chair so that the light of the nearest lamp lit up her face.

"I wish my great-aunt were here," Abby said, sighing. "She'd put it to you straight. I don't know how to do that."

"That's your great-aunt A. Letitia?"

"That's my great-aunt Letty. She's the only great-aunt I have. Uncle Theo's sister. They both shared this old house."

"What would she say?"

Abby chuckled. "You'd better sit down for this, Mr. Farnsworth."

There wasn't another chair in the study. He perched himself on the near corner of the desk and he smiled at her. "All right, I'm ready, Great-Aunt. What is it that you say?"

"Well," said Abby, "my great-aunt Letty would say, 'Young man, just what are you up to? What are your intentions?'"

"Oh, Lord." Selby got up off the corner of the desk. The smile had disappeared. "Am I hearing right?"

"You're hearing right. I—I could not have said it myself, but my great-aunt could have said it easily. Just what are you to me, Selby? And where will we be and what will we be when the next few days have passed? When I go back to work and you go back to the House of Representatives?"

"I——" Plainly he didn't know what to say. He stuttered along as best he could and finally shrugged his shoulders. With a boyish sort of smile he said, "Abby, I don't know what my intentions are. Women are a big mystery to me. I married one, we produced a beautiful son and I never, ever understood her—not for a single minute."

"And she left you?"

"Well—ah—well, yes, in a manner of speaking."

"I don't understand that. What do you mean?"

"Well, when she left she took my bank book. With that in hand, she took out all the money in our joint bank account. She took our only good car and then I didn't hear from her for about six months. At which time, I received notice from her in Las Vegas, Nevada, that she was filing for a divorce. I haven't seen her since."

"I guess you could say that you didn't understand her," Abby said. "Do you miss her?"

Selby struggled with that one, brushing his hand back through his thick hair. "I'm not sure," he said. "Two, three, four years ago I would have said, 'Oh, yes—Lord, I miss her.' But this last few days here on the island, Abby, I haven't missed her a single bit.''

Abby chuckled. ''There's a song about that, isn't there? I've forgotten the name of it but it's something like 'when I can't be near the girl I love then I love the girl I'm near.'''

''Well, mock me if you will,'' he said, ''but I'm having a serious problem. You're a fine woman, Abigail, a very fine woman.''

''Well, I'm pleased that you would say so, kind sir,'' she said, as her heart dropped down into her shoes. A very fine woman? Yes, that's me, Abigail Spencer. A fine figure of a woman—and who would want to marry me? Not Selby Farnsworth! Her smile had long since gone. She whirled around and presented her back to him so he wouldn't see the single tear she could not stop.

''But we've only a few days yet to go.'' She managed to get her voice under control, but barely so. ''Perhaps we can survive to that time. My pick-up boat will be here by the day after tomorrow. Perhaps you could use some of that magic of yours, and get it to come sooner?''

''Me? I don't know how to do that,'' he said. ''I'm just as stuck as you are.'' He came over to her, put his big hands on her shoulders, and turned her around to face him. ''Besides,'' he murmured, ''I wouldn't want to waste a single day with you. They're precious.''

''Yeah, precious,'' she said, and her control snapped. The tears rolled like rain. In her pain she doubled up both fists and beat on his chest with all her feeble strength.

He pulled her close. She buried her tears in his shirt. Both his arms came around her, one hand patting gently in the middle of her back.

"Why, Abby, you're crying." He tilted her chin up and used his handkerchief to wipe her eyes. So I am, she told herself as she snatched the handkerchief and blew her nose, So I am. How did you notice?

When he released her, she stumbled back and fell into the big chair. He went around to the front of the desk, barely visible in the lamplight. Abby stared at his harsh face. He was nibbling on his lower lip as if he hadn't eaten in weeks. A deep furrow ploughed his forehead. I wonder what love really is? she asked herself.

Abby was unable to control the shaking that plagued her arms. She folded them over her breasts and tried her best to retain control. Somehow, something must be done to change the subject. He provided the opportunity. He swung around while gesturing, and sent the two cans on top of the desk rattling into a corner.

"Ah, what's this?" he said, looking around the top of the desk.

"What this is, is a chance to change the subject. Isn't it?" she asked.

"Yes, but," he replied, "look." He picked up the wine bottle. It was dust-covered. She fumbled for something to help him, and could find only his handkerchief. She handed the damp cloth back to him. He wiped the accumulation of dust off the front label. He polished the bottle up in great glee, looking more and more like an explorer scout than ever before. "Would you look at that?" he said.

Yes, Abby told herself. Ten seconds flat and you've completely changed the subject. Ten seconds out of my life. Yes, I'll play your stupid game, Mr. Farnsworth. Why not? There's nothing left of my stupid heart, anyway. "Okay, I'll look at that," Abby said. "Look at what?"

"The wine bottle," he said. "It isn't wine."

"Well, what comes in wine bottles, besides wine?" she said grimly,

"I would think perhaps brandy," he said. "Cognac brandy. Look at this—cognac brandy from France."

"That's nice, I suppose. Is cognac very good to drink?"

"It is probably the tastiest kind of drink that you can get. Especially as it gets older. Look at the date on the bottom of the label—1872."

"Good Lord, that's over a hundred years old."

"Yeah, it surely is." It looked as if Selby was panting, his tongue was out as if he were tasting, his eyes gleamed with high passion. "You don't know what I'm talking about, do you?"

"No, I don't."

"You have here a bottle of prime cognac. More than a hundred years old. Lady, if you had any other ones like this—full—that would be your great-uncle's hidden treasure, believe me."

"Wine?" she said, really not believing it.

"Brandy," he returned. "Now, if the old guy had laid down a cellar full of this cognac, or his father, perhaps, you and I, lady, would be sitting on something worth— oh, a hundred and fifteen dollars per bottle."

Abby took a deep breath. She didn't understand things like a hundred and fifteen dollars a bottle. In fact, when she went out to dinner and had wine, it was usually California at eight dollars. "One bottle?" she asked.

"One bottle. Where in the world would he store something like that, Abby, if he had something like that to store?"

"Why, I don't really know," she said. "There's no real cellar under the house, although there is a crawl space. And somewhere around the back of the house he has a root cellar."

"There's no cellar?" There was a mournful sound to his repeated question.

"No. I'm afraid not. And I don't think my uncle would have stored anything but potatoes in the root cellar. You know, this is a big house, but to my great-uncle Theodore it was strictly a summer cottage!"

"Well, I don't know where anything could be stored," he said, "but I'm eager to look."

At that moment, Harry came wandering in. "Are you two telling secrets?" he asked.

"No, I don't think so," his father said.

The boy looked at Abby sternly. "Have you been kissing my father again?"

Abby stood up and gave him a very stern return. "I'm not kissing your father at the moment. But it if I felt like it I would whether you liked it or not."

"Well," said Harry, "I don't want you making a fuss about it, but I could get used to it if that's what you both want to do. Now what are you up to?"

"How old *is* this child?" Abby demanded.

"You wouldn't believe it if I told you," Selby told her. "At best I can figure he's eight going on eighty. Look, son, we're looking for treasure."

"Treasure?" The boy's face lit up again, as his father's had earlier. "Treasure, treasure!" He pounced around the room doing a funny dance. "Treasure! Where?"

"I don't know," his father said. "Someplace. Someplace in this house, I'll wager?"

"I would suppose so," Abby commented. "Uncle liked to have his treasures close around him. I wouldn't be surprised—if there wasn't some sneaky hiding place right here in this room. As I remember, Uncle Theo hardly used the living room. He spent most of his time here."

Cleo came wandering in the half-opened door. She had heard the ruckus and had come down to join the fun. She managed a few barks, then joined the procession around the room, chasing Harry. Or the other way around with Harry chasing her. It was enough to take Abby's mind off the previous subject, and bring a small smile to her face.

"Shadup!" she shouted. Silence. I'm getting better at it, Abby told herself. When I grow old, I'll have a great advantage. My nephews and nieces will jump at the crack of my tonsils—but Lord, I want my own babies! I don't want to be somebody's maiden aunt! The dark thought threw her back down into her private pit of despair.

"Right in this room?" Selby asked seriously. "There's only one door and that leads out into the hall. Let me— you're sure?"

"I'm—not sure," Abby said. "My mother didn't get along with Uncle Theo, so I didn't spend a great deal of time in this house. But once I heard my great-uncle say that everything he prized the most was here in this room."

"So we look," little Harry said.

And they began to look, so enthusiastically that Abby backed her chair off into a corner and watched. The bookshelves covered three sides of the room, and all the shelves were packed with hardcover books. The shelves were stacked right down to the floor. The pair of them came back to her with questions in their eyes.

"I don't see nothing," Harry said. "Are you sure?"

"I'm not positive," Abby told him. "I didn't know my great-uncle all that well, but that's what he said once. Everything he treasured most was here in this room."

"Got an awful lot of books," Harry said.

"Nothing except books," Selby interjected. "And all of them published before the turn of the century. Was your great-uncle a voracious reader?"

"Now that's a good question," Abby returned. "I don't believe that in all the years that I knew him I ever saw him read anything other than the *Wall Street Journal* and the *Daily Racing Form*."

"Well, that's a surprise," Selby said softly. 'He's got more books in here than you could carry on the *Titanic*——"

"What's the *Titanic*?" Harry interrupted.

"Oh, shadup," Selby said, but he was laughing as he did so. He ruffled the boy's hair. "It's none of your business what the *Titanic* was. Now, then—everything that he prized the most is here in this room. He didn't read anything much and you've got three walls' worth of bookcases all filled to the——"

"What are you thinking?" Harry asked.

"I'm thinking of one of the finest detective stories ever written," Selby said. "By a Frenchman, a long time ago. Where do you hide something securely? In plain sight." He walked over to the right-hand corner of the bookcase and began to lay the books down so that whatever was behind them could be seen. He went all the way across the room on that one side, so that the books were now all lying down on their spines, and the area behind them was uncovered. It was as dusty as any other part of the room and there was nothing to be seen.

"Hide it in plain sight?" Abby asked. "That must be one whale of a story. Are you going to write that some time?"

"What did you say?"

"I said are you——? Whoops!" He's a writer, and *he* knows it. I know he's a writer. He thinks I don't know that, she thought frantically.

"What do you know about me writing books?" he said. He came over to her chair and leaned over so that she was forced to lie back and look up at him.

"I don't know a great deal about your writing books," she said. "I suppose they're—what? Detective stories?"

"Tell me some more," he said in that confident tone with those steel eyes watching her.

"Why, I'm afraid I can't tell you a thing," she said. "I claim the Fifth Amendment."

"Daddy?" Harry called. They both turned around. The boy was at the bookcase, barely able to reach the first shelf. Now a whole line of books were on the floor and there, staring them straight in the eye, was a doorknob.

"Oh, boy. That's all we need," Selby said. "It reminds me of our third Christmas. I bought a whole bunch of toys advertised by the store to be suitable for children of the ages two to eight. Any eight-year old could put them together, the advertisement said. Unfortunately, I didn't have an eight-year-old available. I finally had to go out on the streets to find one."

"I'm gonna turn the knob, Daddy," said Harry.

"So you're going to turn the knob," Selby said. "Turn."

The boy reached up and tugged the knob and pulled back on it. It squeaked and groaned and as it did so a crack developed in what had seemed to be a solid backing. At the same time the books stacked in the racks directly above where the boy was working were pushed off the bookcase and thundered to the floor.

Harry squealed in excitement, even though two of the tomes had landed on his head. "Will you look at that?" Selby commented. Row after row of wine bottles stared him in the face. He reached carefully up to the top shelf, and took down one bottle. He rubbed his hand across the bottom of the label.

"1872," he said in awe. On the middle shelf, "1874." On the bottom shelf, "1876. Oh! Was *that* ever a good year for cognac!"

"What have we got?" Harry said. The boy was dancing up and down, trying to control himself. "Dirty Coca-Cola?"

"I'm afraid not," his father told him. "It's something worth more than that, love." He took another bottle down. Behind it in the rack was another layer of bottles. "Good Lord," he said again, sounding very religious. As he went down the whole line of books he picked them off the shelf and passed them one at a time to little Harry. The child, chortling all the while, immediately dropped each one on the floor. More doors, more counting. It took more than thirty minutes to count everything and when Selby came back to Abby, still sitting in her corner, her mouth half open in surprise, he said, "Four hundred and twenty-five bottles of one-hundred-year-old brandy, lady."

Good Lord, she said to herself. Good Lord. It seemed to be the only phrase she could muster. The only one that fitted all the circumstances.

"Is that good, Daddy?" Harry said.

"That's great," he returned. "That's great. Miss Abby Spencer is worth a whole lot of money."

"Wow," Harry said. "And all in old dusty bottles."

"Well, we didn't have to dig 'em up, right?"

"Yeah, that's right," Harry said. "But it would have been more fun to dig 'em up."

"Let's be practical," Abby said. "We can't drink it all, so let's close up the cabinets and go have lunch."

They were in the kitchen at the usual table for lunch. There was more on the menu this time. The refrigerator contained more eggs than Abby knew what to do with, so she made omeletes for each of them. There was cold, fresh milk. There was a tossed salad, which she concocted offhandedly, as if she really knew what it was all about. Her conscience bothered her on that one. It had really been more luck than skill.

"You're quite a cook, aren't you?" Selby said.

"Now don't get your hopes up on that," Abby said. "I'm not a great cook, I'm a competent cook. Now my mother—she is a *great* cook."

"Umm," Selby said.

"Hey," Harry butted in, "if you was to marry my daddy, could your mother come live with us?"

"Closet love," Abby said. "What are you thinking of? Whoever said anything about me marrying your daddy?" She could feel her face burn with the blush that had risen. Selby could see it all plainly exposed. Good Lord, she thought. Abigail Spencer, you are one great fool. You've fallen in love with the man and with his son. This was the first time she had admitted that fact to herself in as many words.

That was the moment that there came a tremendous knock at the front door.

"What can that be?" said Harry, showing the same surprised look that his father always used.

"I don't know," Abby returned, but before she could say anything else the boy had gone. He scooted out of the kitchen door, down the hall, tooting like a fire engine as he went. He struggled with the big door and before either of the two adults could get within range he had pulled it open, and there were three rain-soaked men in yellow rain gear, all trying to get into the shelter of the tiny triangular roof that covered the porch.

"Come in," Abby said. "Come in out of the wet!"

And in they came.

"Ma'am?" A very nice young man he was. He looked to be about twenty-two—well, maybe twenty-three. The man with him could, perhaps, be his father. Behind them—well, she really didn't have time to look at the moment.

"Yes, what can I do for you all?" she said.

"We're the coast guard representatives, ma'am," the young fellow said. "I'm Lieutenant Janus, and this is CPO Franklin. We've—uh—are you the—er—do you own this island——?" He turned to look at Selby, an almost natural instinct.

Abby giggled under her breath. The power of mankind, she said to herself. All *men* are created equal, and then there are women.

"I'm the owner of the island," she interrupted.

The young man turned to her with a blush. "I'm sorry, ma'am," he said. "We have a report from Cutty Hunk that a small runabout, which evidently broke loose from its mooring a few days ago, has turned up on the rocks on the far side of Cutty Hunk. We weren't sure whether it had passengers and—what can you tell us about it?" As he finished his statement he looked at his chief petty officer for approval. The CPO nodded.

"It was my boat," Abby said. "I leased it for fifteen days. It broke loose, as you say, and we had no way to get it back."

"You don't have any other boats?"

"No, no."

"You don't have a telephone?"

"No."

"You don't have a radio?"

"No."

"Well, you certainly gave us a frustrating week," the young officer said. "All right, I'll write it all down and we'll make a report to coast guard headquarters in

Boston. You really have to take more care if you're living on an island like this one."

"Not to worry," Selby said. "The next time I'll be sure she brings along a radio."

"Would you care to stay for a while?" Abby offered. "It's a terrible storm out there." Stay long enough for me to calm down, Abby thought. That arrogant damn man, taking me over as if I were one of his possessions. If I'm alone with Selby Farnsworth for longer that two minutes I'm going to get out my butcher's knife and shorten him—someplace.

"It won't get any better," the coastguardsman said. "Not a chance."

The third man, who had been standing behind them all this time, in the gloom of the hall, forced his way forward. "You remember me, lady? Harrelson from the *Providence Gazette*," he said. "Mr. Farnsworth, I'd like to——"

There's a time to explode, and a time to rake grass, Abby told herself. And with me this is explosion time. "Get out of my house," she commanded. "I told you that once before!"

"What? Look, all I want to know, Mr.——"

"Get out of my house," Abby repeated. Her face was red, but this was with anger. She balled up her fists and presented them for inspection. "Why did you bring this—person, with you? Is he a part of the coast guard?"

"You mean Harrelson?" the coastguardsmsan said. "No. We were coming out anyway, and it's a common courtesy to offer a ride to people who have to get out among these islands."

"It may be common courtesy to you, Lieutenant, but this man is totally unacceptable to me," Abby said.

"He's a reporter and he's a snake! I *don't* want him in my house. Get out!"

"Listen, this will get you nowhere," the reporter said. "I got it all down. This is Representative Farnsworth and there's his kid——"

"His boy," Abby interrupted. "Boy. He's not a 'kid.'"

"Well, here's his boy and here are you. Now what I need to know is—who are you? Are you his ladybird?"

"Get—out—of—my—house," Abby said. Each word was stated distinctly, frozen like a train of icicles, and ending in what sounded like a whip cracking. "Harry, go down to the kitchen and bring me back my broom."

The reporter took one or two steps backward. The coastguardsman said, "I'm sorry, ma'am, I didn't realize we'd be causing you any problems."

"He's a problem that I don't care to share with anybody," Abby said. "I thank you for your concern for us and I wish you'd go and take this man with you— away from here. And if he is ever on my island again I'm going to shoot him. Cleo, Cleo."

The old dog had been lying down, sleeping in the middle of the study. She opened one eye gradually, pushed herself to her feet and struggled out into the corridor. She evidently remembered the smell of the reporter as she immediately fell into her hunting crouch. Sliding across the floor, belly down, feet slipping one at a time, growling, she once again advanced on the reporter.

"All right," said Harrelson, "I'm going, I'm going. But you'll be sorry for this."

"I bet I will," said Abby. "And the next time I see you it will be in court. Out of here."

"In that case, we'll have to take him back. Thank you, ma'am. It's been a pleasure knowing that good has come from all this. God bless."

"Well, what a nice young man," Abby said, but she had the sense to wait until he was out of the door. "What a lovely young man."

Selby came up beside her and put one arm around her waist. "I'm afraid," he said slowly, "that that was a bad mistake, Abby."

CHAPTER SEVEN

THE day which had begun at a new low got continually worse toward evening. At about eight o'clock Abby found herself sitting in the living room on the massive couch. There were a few flames left in the fireplace. She added a couple of logs and then sat and gazed into it. The blue flames of the sea wood flickered, almost teasing her into a hypnotic state.

Harry was upstairs in bed. His father was upstairs too, evidently telling something in the order of a Popodopolis story. For just a second, Abby felt discouraged, as if her copyright and her mind had been violated at the same time. By the time the wall clock struck nine everything was quiet from the upper floor.

Cleo came shuffling into the room, looking for a little loving. Abby put both feet flat on the floor, because she knew what was coming. The big dog wanted to sleep and be close all at the same time. In the stillness of the night Abby could hear the asthmatic breathing. Good old dog, Abby thought, as the animal draped her eighty pounds across both of Abby's feet. Good old dog?

The thought startled her. It had been more years than she hated to remember. All that friendship and warmth and love can't last forever, Abby Spencer, she lectured herself. Brothers and mother and dad she had, but none was as close to her as Cleo—who was growing old. Love is fleeting. Nagged by the unwelcome thought, Abby reached over and ruffled Cleo's fur just behind her ears.

Things were so quiet in the house that she could hear the wall clock ticking and the wood snapping in the fireplace. Somehow, unnoticed, the storm had fled, but clouds still blotted out the stars. It is certainly dismal, she told herself as she pulled the couch blanket over her knees. Cleo grumbled at the disturbance and squirmed around to reestablish herself in comfort. Or maybe it's just me, Abby told herself. Why am I so confused? I'm caught up in a simple situation. I'm marooned on an island with a man and a boy. Marooned? A poor choice of words, lady. All you need to do is get out your telephone and make a call. You could be rescued by tomorrow noon.

Another poor choice of words. Rescued! It's almost the last thing in the world you want—to be rescued. Idiot! You're not the prettiest girl in the world, but you expect this short acquaintance to blossom into love? Some imagination, chum. He's a man of the world. A congressman, a novelist, and a lawyer. Why would he want to play around with poor little you? It was a sarcastic question, and deserved a sarcastic answer. Idiot! You're the only female on the island, and probably he just hates to get out of practice! So turn off your stupid mind and relax.

She crossed her arms, leaned back against the couch and stared into the fire. Moments later, Selby came down the stairs. He was doing his best to be silent, but she could trace the movement of his shoes over the risers of the stairs. Looking over her shoulder, she could see the dim shadow of his movements. It's hard, she told herself, for a two-hundred-pound man to steal down an old squeaky staircase.

When he got to the foot of the stairs, he called softly, "Abby? Which way did you go?"

"In the living room, Selby," she said quietly.

Moments later, he was with her, going cautiously in the firelight. He stumbled once over the leg of the couch.

Cleo groaned a complaint. Selby managed to find the other end of the couch and sat down, perhaps an inch or two from Abby. Cleo whined disgustedly, stretched herself up, and marched doggedly over to the warmth of the hearthstone.

"Mesmerizing, isn't it?" Selby murmured.

"Hmm?"

"The flame. The wood. Mesmerizing. This is what our great-grandparents used before TV came along, you know. Everybody would sit and watch shapes in the flames. Seen anybody you know?"

"Oh, stop it," Abby muttered. "I don't feel very cheery."

"Well, poor you." And then he gave up the sarcasm and became sympathetic. "It's been a difficult day, hasn't it?"

"You never said a truer word," Abby replied. There was a moment or two of quiet. Cleo clumped her heavy tail on the floor once or twice, making it sound like a bass drum. There was an extra warmth that Abby hadn't expected, as Selby moved that inch closer, put his arm around her and with the free hand toyed with her ear.

"Why do you do that?" she asked, driven by the devils of curiosity.

"Because I want to," he said. "I'd like to lean over there and bite you on your ear—and a lot of other places as well."

"I wish—I wish you wouldn't. I'm not on the menu."

"No? Are you sure?"

"As sure as I can be. That's why I wear these big earrings. I do it just so that strange men can't bite my ears."

"Strange? After all this time? I thought we had become fairly close."

Happy for the semidarkness that hid her blush, she struggled for an answer and found none.

"Abby Spencer," he said, after a moment of silence, "you are some kind of a spoilsport."

Abby mulled that over for a minute. Maybe he's right, she thought. I haven't done anything outstandingly wonderful on this dark day. But biting ears was not exactly a safe subject.

"Tell me some more about Harry," she said. "How come he isn't in school already? Most of the schools in Massachusetts start one or two days after Labor Day, in early September."

"For one thing," he said, "Harry is enrolled in a school for advanced children. It doesn't open until September twentieth, and it runs until the day before Christmas. The rest of the year is independent study with a tutor. Believe me, he learns more than I'd care for him to know in that short time. The Morgenstern School for Advanced Children—have you ever heard of it?"

"No, I can't say that I have," she said. "We have a big family. The only kind of advances we got in our family were when Daddy passed out a little pocket money on occasion. He's that smart, your boy?"

"He's smarter than that," Selby said, sighing. "Have you ever known a time when you have to be careful when you're speaking to a child, because he or she might very well know more than you do?"

"No, I've never had that problem." Abby nestled back into the couch and found that she was resting her head on his arm and he was moving just that inch closer. She could feel the heat of his thigh as it pressed against hers. She stiffened her mind against it. It wasn't the least bit odious, but it could be dangerous. "What's Harry's legal status now? You said before that your wife—your former wife—had custody, yet here he is."

"A change of plan," he reported. "My *former* wife found that no matter how much money I gave her she still couldn't support the boy and entertain all the male friends she's made. So, with permission of the court, I am now temporarily Harry's sole guardian."

And that's too much information for my feeble mind, Abby told herself, and then changed the subject. "It's stopped raining. Why don't we take a walk?"

"Changing the subject?" His chuckle was deep-seated. It sent a little shiver up Abby's spine, as if someone were scratching his or her nails on a blackboard.

"Not changing the subject," she argued. "Just changing the—what is that lawyer word? Venue?"

"One more for your side." He came up to his feet in one graceful surge, and towed her along by the arm. Cleo, across the room at the hearth, raised her heavy head and stared.

"We're going walking," Abby told the dog. "Do you want to come?"

The wise old animal shook her head, stretched out again on the warm bricks of the hearth, and closed her eyes.

"So much for us, huh?" Selby looked down at her. It might have been the colored flames from the fireplace, Abby thought, but at the moment he really looks like some sort of devil. Oh, well.

They walked side by side to the front door and looked out. A few high clouds raced across the sky, silhouetted in the light of a half-moon. The stars were bright—and close. The wind dropped to a murmur. Nothing could be seen other than navigation lights and the glow of civilization on the Cape, just across the channel. Somehow, without her realizing, his arm was around her shoulders, and her arm was around his waist. They moved slowly down the hill in lock-step.

"Lovely moon," Selby said softly. "Moon, June, honeymoon?"

"You struck out early," she returned, with a lilt in her voice. "It's September already, and I don't see much——" She stopped talking, having just tripped over her tongue. And I don't see much chance for a honeymoon, she was about to say. "Selby, do you suppose people can really fall in love at first sight?"

"Anything's possible." It was too dark for her to read his facial expression, but his grip tightened on her shoulders.

"Yes, but——" She paused again to refine her question. "You've had much more experience at that sort of thing than I have. I don't even know what 'love' means."

"Dictionary words? Love is a tender affection for someone. As the Bible says, 'Love thy neighbor.'"

"That can't be all there is to it." Her voice sounded her discouragement.

"Now if you mean between man and woman," he reflected, "there must be a great deal more. Fixation, for one thing. Have you ever seen a newly born duck? Whatever comes across its line of sight when it opens its eyes—that the duckling notes down as his mother. And the little guy will stick to that idea until hell won't have it. I suspect there's something of that nature in human love."

"But it doesn't happen to everyone."

"I know. You have to add other ingredients. Compassion, long-term affection, passion. I don't know what else. Oh, yes, I do. You have to really *like* someone in order to be in love with them."

They walked slowly on, avoiding the grass areas which were still wet from the rain. "You don't say anything?"

"I—I don't dare," she said, sighing. The list ran through her mind. Fixation? Yes, she certainly had that. Almost from the first day they had met. Compassion? I don't know what that means—unless it deals with his problem and Harry. Passion? She hardly knew the word. Oh, there had been some wild petting dates in her high school years, but only one that went beyond the proprieties—and that one had hurt her so much that she had never given the subject another chance to develop.

"Selby, do you ever think that—some day—you might marry again?"

"Yes. Often. But I'd have to explain. Harry is a wonderful kid, who just happened to be born to a pair of lousy parents. Whatever I do about marriage depends almost completely on Harry's needs, not mine. He misses his mother—a lot more than I do, I'll tell you. But if that's the way the cookie crumbles that's what I'll do."

He gave her shoulder another little squeeze that brought them to a halt. And then he said cynically, "Besides, that would reduce my alimony payments, and maybe I wouldn't have to struggle with three different jobs."

"Ah. That's why you need the money."

"You're so right," he said. "Our divorce judge out in Las Vegas was very liberal in giving away my money."

"And going back to her is the only way it could be cut down?"

"Well, not the only way," he replied. "If I can get her to marry that clown she left with, then all the bonds are broken. The day she gets married is the last day I pay alimony."

"It sounds very—mercenary," she told him. They had come full circle around the hill, and were standing on the dock. She turned her head away and let the rising wind ruffle her hair. Her eyes were watering. Because of the wind, she told herself. I'm not crying, damn it! I'm not!

Her toe caught on a piece of line lying on the dock, and she tripped. Before she could fall completely he had her in his arms, pulling her around so that they were face-to-face. His finger traced the fall of the tears down her cheek.

"What's all this? Too serious a discussion?"

"No—I was just—curious." She turned around, still in the circle of his arms, body pressed back against him and enjoying his warmth. "What did you want to be——?"

"If I ever grew up?"

"Well, something like that."

"I think I would want to take Harry back to Ohio. We have a farm out there, with lots of acreage. It hasn't shown a profit in twenty years or more, but I have some ideas about that. But that's enough about me. What about you?"

"I don't know, Selby. I'm not really an ambitious woman. I know for sure that I don't want to continue what I do now."

"And what is that?"

Foot in the mouth again, she told herself. Snap to it, woman! "I—have a very minor position on a newspaper. I wouldn't want to—— I guess I'm a throwback. I'd like to marry a man and live in the country, and have three or four children, and——"

"And live happily ever after?"

She whirled around again and glared up at him. There was just enough moonlight to see that his face was solemn. The tension dropped. Her arms relaxed, and she hung on to his arms for a moment.

"Yes," she said in a half whisper. "And live happily ever after. Let's go back to the house, shall we?"

"Tired of walking so soon?"

"I have a dozen things on my mind," she told him. Well, only one, she thought. Only one. I've got them all. Tenderness, compassion, liking, affection, fixation. But what about passion? She was still debating the subject as they came into the living room. Cleo squeezed one eye open, gave them a ten-second look, and went back to sleep.

He maneuvered her back onto the couch, and crowded so close that she could almost feel his heartbeat. "So tell me about Harry," she offered.

"Well, let me tell you it's no fun trying to raise a kid whose Intelligence Quotient is twenty-five points above your own. When I was nine years old I felt put upon when the teacher demanded we memorize the times table. You know, one times one, two times two?" She offered him a sympathetic nod. "Well, my kid is already studying calculus."

"Makes you sort of sick to your stomach?"

"It doesn't do much for my ego, either," he replied.

Cleo interrupted with a groan, rolled over a time or two and then went off to sleep again. "She doesn't like people to be jabbering while she's napping," Abby explained.

"Nice dog," Selby said.

"Yes, but she didn't go to an advanced school," Abby babbled, not knowing what else to say. "She's about as dumb as they come, but we all love her. She wasn't my dog originally, you know. She belonged to my oldest brother, and then the next brother, and the next, and then, finally, she belonged to me. I guess we're the runts of the family, so to speak."

"I wouldn't say that," he said. Somehow or other he had got so close that she was leaning partially on his chest, the top of her head just under his chin. It wasn't a bad feeling, not at all. In fact, Abby instructed herself, you know the score. He doesn't love you. He's been stung once before in the marriage game, and he's told you flat out that he's not playing that again. But it's warm and cozy, a long way from my editor and Selby's political party. So nice—and you might not get as good an offer in the next ten years. There's something to be said for lust. With which, she tucked her conscience away down deep in the back of her mind and moved over to lean fully against him.

"Ah," he said, "that's nice."

"Yes, isn't it?" she returned sleepily.

He moved down the couch a bit, eased her head down into his lap, and swung her feet up so they were resting on the arm of the sofa. "Now how's that?"

"That's pretty good," she said breathlessly. One of his hands was toying with her hair. The other had moved cautiously down the hill of her left breast, and came to a gentle stop just under its upward curve.

Leave things alone, her devils told her. She compromised by placing one of her own hands on top of his, and changed the subject.

"Do you have any other tricks? Do you do acrobatic stunts? Why did you get so mad when I told the reporter to get out of here?"

"Well, that's a delicate political matter," he said. His voice was soft and deep and as hypnotic as the flames. "Did you know I was a politician?"

"I didn't before that reporter showed up," she said, "but I found out your secret and sank his boat. Is there anything else you are? You don't own an undertaking establishment, perhaps, or a ten-piece band?"

"No, nothing like that," he said. "Nothing like that. The political sense of all this, Abby, is that when reporters think they have a political scalp they can collect they all gather like a horde of wolves and bark at you until you say something you don't want to say. These days, in politics, a member of congress is expected to be like Caesar's wife."

"Which one?" Abby asked in all innocence. "He had two. One was Pompey's daughter, and the other was Cleopatra. And, come to think of it, congressmen these days are worse than either of them."

"Thanks a lot," he grumbled. "We're all human. Some are worse than others. This high-pressure work leads to a lot of stress, and a great many divorces. What was I saying?"

"Caesar's wife," she teased.

"Yeah. Caesar's wife. And when the media find some little chink in your armor they write you up for the national Press. They try to hang you out to dry. The story appears in the newspapers in big bold print—not only in Washington, but back home in the district, where people read *and* vote. So a congressman has to learn early in the game to be a darned sight more circumspect with reporters than we are with real people."

"Well, I'm sorry about that," Abby said, with a little tremor in her voice. His hand had moved an inch or two higher, and was gently weighing her capacious breast. "I haven't any of that kind of experience, you must realize. To me, a large audience is three people when I play the piano at home."

"That's your mother, your dad and yourself?"

"No. That's my mother and dad and Cleo. All the boys have married and established their own homes. But Cleo listens all the time. My dog thinks I'm wonderful. Don't you, Cleo?" The animal lifted her heavy head, shook it until her ears began to fall out, and then put her nose back down on the hearth again. "You see what I mean," Abby said. "Total loyalty. So what about it?

What about this reporter thing? Do you think they'll come back?''

"I know they'll come back. In fact, I'd be surprised if we don't have a real gathering tomorrow. The only thing that could keep them out, I guess, is the possibility of a hurricane. Did you suppose that reporters are like other people? Other people would come to the coast, take a look at the size of the waves and decide not to make the trip. Not reporters. You don't find them saying, I'll go tomorrow, or the next day, or the day after that. Not a chance. When they smell blood they come running. Yes, I do expect them to come back tomorrow."

She felt that wandering hand again, rising to the peak of the mountain and fastening on the hardened bronze tip. She had forgotten a bra this morning when she was dressing. Purposefully? It was hard to breathe; hard to suppress that delicate little moan.

"I don't expect that my being here is going to help," Abby finally said. "That—man—asked me if I were your new ladybird. What do you suppose he meant by that?"

"Just what you think he meant," Selby said. "I'm mulling over a story to tell them. One that will protect your reputation as well as my own."

That startled Abby. She had not given a thought to her *own* reputation. She almost sat up, but the weight of his arm prevented it. And now his exploring hand had moved up to find the V-shape of her *décolletage*, and slipped inside. Conversation was suspended for the moment. The little moan was real. Her whole body squirmed. His fingers caressed her overheated skin, then withdrew to toil with the buttons of her blouse. Moving as slowly and surely as volcano lava, he slipped three of the fastenings. She could feel the sudden coolness, and then the overheating as her breast fell into his cupped hand and was gently kneaded. Her whole body shivered, not from the cold but from anticipation. Get control of yourself, she demanded as she strained all her muscles to combat the invasive feeling.

"Some kind of lie?" she managed to gasp.

"Oh, come on, now. You're making a big thing out of that," Selby said. "So I do tell a few whoppers here and there. I have to think of something, don't I? These people could blast me right out of my career with one story in the papers. Can't you see the headline? Congressman Selby Farnsworth who is supposedly in the House voting for or against the agriculture bill is, instead, found shacked up on an island——"

"What? Shacked up? What's that mean?"

"It's—you don't need to know what that means, Abby. Well, anyway, they'll find Congressman Farnsworth out on this island with a beautiful woman and his own little boy, playing house. And that story will go out on all the wires, all the networks and, even though I haven't a great name in the congress, they'll make the story a major crime. The next thing I'll get is a summons from the majority whip, and then—who knows?—out in the cornfields for me."

"Hmm—do you like the job?"

"Yes, I like the job," he said. And all the time his fingers were kneading, stroking, as he caught her nipple between his thumb and forefinger. His voice was as firm and clear as it ever had been. Every time Abby tried to answer she had to clear her throat.

"I don't intend to have it for long," he said. "I thought to run for three terms—six years—and then leave it for somebody else. There are some things I want to do. After six years I suspect I'll be all out of new ideas, so I'll make room for a younger man.

"I like the job," he continued. "I hope to keep it. I won't if these reporters come up here and don't find a perfect answer for all their myriad questions."

His hand had stilled. It rested, warm, heavy and comforting, but not moving. It gave her enough strength to continue. "What are you telling me? They'll come tomorrow?"

"Of course."

"Well, I——"

"Hush," he said. He shifted her body and leaned over to catch her exposed nipple between his lips. It was a feeling she had never met with before. Her breast rose to meet him as he gently suckled. All her muscles screamed to attention. One of her hands went up and tangled in his hair. He started to withdraw; she held him to the work. His hand moved to uncover her other breast. He toyed with it while his tongue teased gently where it was. She moaned.

Cleo snapped her head up and growled, then, deciding nothing was amiss, dropped back into her slumbers. Selby lifted his head. "Am I hurting you?"

"No," she whispered as she pulled him back down by the hair. He went willingly.

They stayed on the couch for a time longer. They had nothing really to say. They were doing a lot of things that they might not have done back home, and it was pleasant. Not until the wall clock struck twelve did Abby stir, shake herself, and push herself away from this tremendously muscled man and stand up. He watched as she refastened her blouse with suddenly clumsy fingers. "I think it's time to go to bed," she said.

He sighed. "I don't suppose that's an invitation," he said.

"I—what do you mean?" Abby asked, moving a step or two away from him.

"Well, we could go to bed together."

Abby flushed, not knowing what to say. So as her mind fumbled she said, "I don't—have a great deal of experience. I——"

"Hell, Abby! There's no need to defend yourself," he said as he came up off the couch in one single smooth motion. "I have the feeling that you haven't had any experience at all."

She turned away from him to hide the blush. 'I—I——" she stuttered. "No, I don't have—no." A pause restored the silence of the night. She shrugged herself into her blouse. The conversation was not yet complete, but she hardly knew what to say. Finally, she just took her courage in her hands and turned to face him, holding herself as stiffly as a sentry on guard. "It's true. I'm twenty-nine years old and I have no experience at all, but that doesn't mean that I want to continue that way, especially when I'm with a man whom I admire and trust and—would you?"

There. It was out. No word about love and devotion. He had none of that to give. But she had plenty. And if there was only to be one occasion in her life she wanted it to be here and now with Selby. "Would you?"

He caught her up in his arms. She buried her head in his chest, and waited.

"Not like some virgin sacrifice," he muttered. "If you feel the wanting as much as I do, we'll do it. If not——"

"Good God!" she exclaimed. "I'm on fire!"

"Then we'll go up," he said, and put an arm around her to guide her to the stairs. Cleo raised her head again, and watched them go out into the hall. The old dog must have decided that things were all right. She squirmed a couple of times, shifted her position, and went back to sleep. Abby, noticing her dog's defection, felt somewhat like the Roman slave going to the block alone, and crossed her fingers for good luck.

Her bedroom was dark. Selby guided her to the bed, and then fumbled at the side table until a tiny lamp was lit, about the size of a night-light.

"Isn't it—best done in darkness?" she whispered, shivering.

"Not at all," he said, chuckling. "There are a thousand ways of doing this. I prefer some light."

"A thousand and one? Scheherazade?"

"Don't let yourself be carried away, Abby. There's nothing wrong or shameful about it. If you believe that God created man and woman, you have to believe He created this. Now sit here on the bed. I have to go down to my room to get some protection for us both."

She opened her mouth and snapped it shut without asking. You would have to be both dumb and blind, she lectured herself, without having seen how it's done. Almost every movie on television in these days and times gave an almost graphic portrayal.

Yes, but, her Calvinist mind retorted, seeing others do it in a movie is not the same as doing it yourself. You don't even know how to start!

Your mother was supposed to tell you all about this years ago, her devils argued. All the little details. But she didn't, Abby protested. She was too busy raising boys, or too shy to get to it, or——

Or what? Surely *he* knows what to do! He's been married, and he has a son, and if that doesn't make him an expert—— All I have to do is lie down on the bed and—and maybe he's not all that expert, she lectured grimly. Maybe he only did it once, and didn't get it right, and that's why he's divorced?

There wasn't time for more debate. She could hear him moving quietly up the corridor. He stopped next door—to check on Harry, she supposed. I hope the kid's fast asleep. Like a rock he should sleep. What could be more embarrassing than to have him find his father and me in the middle—of it? And then there he was, coming into her room, turning to shut the door quietly but securely behind him. And turning to her.

"Why are you so pale?"

"Oh—I'm not really pale. I just tend to look that way in lamplight," she stammered. "It—I——" And then one accusatory tear broke loose and ran down her face. "I've only done it once before—and it hurt," she wailed.

"So I'll show you," he assured her, and his voice was deep and sympathetic. "And it won't hurt, believe me." He sat down beside her on the bed. The springs sagged, throwing her against him. His arm came around her shoulders, steadying her. Her head was bent; she peeped up at him through the screen of her eyelashes. He was smiling.

"Don't you dare laugh at me!"

"Laugh at you? This isn't a laughing matter," he assured her. A moment of silence. He pushed himself back to lie flat on the sheets, and took her with him. His hand tangled in her hair, pulling out the two bobby pins that fastened what was left of her chignon. She made no protest. It seemed to be the thing to do—although why they couldn't do it with hairpins in her hair she wasn't quite sure.

He rolled over, half on top of her. His weight startled her, but the long, searching kiss did more. For a moment she stiffened. "Relax," he murmured. She obeyed. His tongue searched her lips, penetrated into her own mouth, touched her tongue.

See, she told herself frantically, all you have to do is whatever he tells you. But he didn't say anything else, and her hands were surrounding his head, pulling it down harder and closer, and there seemed to be something wrong with her breathing. And his too, for that matter.

He was gliding his kiss down from her lips, over the cliff of her chin, and down into the sensitive valley of her throat. His hand reached for the buttons of her blouse; she had already unfastened them all. He brushed the cloth aside even while she was congratulating herself for knowing to undo them beforehand. See, she told herself fiercely. I'm not all that dumb——

And then his nibbling tongue arrived at the tip of her breast, and fires broke out all over her nervous system. She moaned as he flattened her on the bed, holding her down by sheer weight. He attacked both of her high-peaked breasts with hand and tongue of fire. She welcomed the attack wordlessly. No, she assured herself in one brief second of cognition, there's nothing at all laughable about this!

There came a time when a couple played this teasing game when all sense was lost in the pursuit of pleasure. With Abby, it came sooner than later. And when he temporarily rolled away from her she felt bereft.

"Only a minute, love," he said.

She shaded her eyes to follow his movements as he stripped. The last time she had seen a male completely nude was ten years ago, she recalled, and the boy had been her own age. She wasn't sure what course to take—hide her eyes, or watch. So she compromised, putting both hands over her eyes and peeking between the interstices of her fingers.

Until that moment, he had been working on known ground—herself and her body. But now a new element had entered into the game. He was slim and muscled, and—'Oh, my God,'' she muttered—and so big! She closed her fingers tightly against each other and held her breath.

He came back again, as promised, down on the bed beside her, bringing the warmth, the passion, the excitement with him. Somehow her blouse had gone down the wind. Her skirt fastened on the side, and he evidently had a road map of the whole area. She felt another touch of cold air, but it wasn't the air that made her shiver. One of his hands came back to toy with her breast, adding flame to the fire. The other touched at her waist, and for one stupid moment she could not see why—until he tugged at her briefs, and whisked them away like magic.

"But—why?" she moaned, and his fingers showed her why. Abby was perspiring madly; so was he. He shifted his body upward to kiss her again, nibble on her earlobe, and come back down to those vulnerable breasts, nuzzling at their sensitive tips, kneading their softness. She writhed, trying madly to pull him down on her, closer, but he had his own ideas. One of his hands disappeared, riding down across her stomach. She took a surprisingly deep breath, but the hand kept moving downward until it dived off the precipice of her groin and landed on just that one spot in the heart of her femininity. She could not hold back on the scream of delight, and struggled to trap him forever between her legs.

"Slow and easy. This won't hurt," he said as he pushed her legs apart and presented himself. His approach was gentle, but it *was* only the second time for her, and he was a man of great parts, so when finally he leaned forward and entered her fully she shuddered at the expected pain—but there was none, and he was riding her and she was welcoming him and the world was revolving in her mind, spiraling up to the greatest physical enjoyment that man and woman could enjoy, until she felt the coming of the Little Death, and he brought it home by a massive stroke and they both collapsed against each other, feeling a little sad as the pleasures peaked and ran away into nothing.

"Good lord," she gasped. He raised himself up and wiped her forehead with a tissue from the bedside table.

"There," he said, and started to roll off her.

Her arms went around him. "No," she said dreamily. "Not yet."

He dropped back down on her, spreading his welcome weight across her pelvis.

She reordered her mind. It had been like riding the highest and fastest roller coaster in the world, and parts of her being were still scattered back there along the tracks. She took a deep breath, and hugged him madly. And that, she told herself, is that. I've plenty of passion—well, with this man and for this man. And now the only thing left is to get Harry's permission.

"Would you like——?" he started to say.

"Mommy," the little boy cried. He was out on the stairwell again, wailing for his mother.

"Harry," Selby muttered as he rolled away from her and fumbled for something to cover himself with. She was faster. Her robe was draped over the chair next to the bed, and she was into it and out of the door before he could snatch a sheet from the bed and wrap it around him.

Harry was cuddled up against the newel post, not exactly crying, but so close to it as made no difference. Abby sat down beside him, and the moment he felt her warmth he turned away from the cold wood and threw himself across her lap, scrabbling to get closer.

"Mommy," he said, sighing. Abby tucked him into the corner of her elbow, and used her other hand to rub his back.

"Did something disturb you, Harry?" she whispered.

"Mommy," he said, in a very satisfied tone. And by that time Selby was there beside her.

"Your mother's not here," he told the boy. "But if you want her so badly I'll get her back for you." He sounded as if the words were tearing at his heart. "She's down in Washington, you know."

The little boy raised his head, his eyes sparkling, but not fully awake. And there, Abby told herself, goes my last chance. He'll take his wife back because the boy needs her.

"Is that what you want?" Selby asked.

"I want my mommy," the boy insisted as he dropped back over the edge toward sleep. "I want my mommy." With that, he threw his arms around Abby's neck, pressing his soft child's face into hers, and went promptly back to sleep. Abby's heart went slamming down into her feet. What Harry wants, Harry gets, she told herself morosely.

Selby walked around them, picked up his son, and carried him away. Abby remained on the stair step, huddled up as miserably as a woman could get, having just discovered that all the sweets in the candy store were made of plasterboard and paint.

CHAPTER EIGHT

MORNING came gently. Abby came back to the real world slowly. Her bedroom door creaked open, and she heard the patter of Cleo's feet on the hardwood floor. The dog came across to the bed, breathing heavily. Abby kept her eyes closed, but could not suppress a tiny smile. Cleo came up on her hind legs, swaying the bed as she dropped her forelegs onto it. She sniffed a couple of times, then used her rough tongue to lick her mistress's nose. "It's time to get up," the dog said.

Both of Abby's eyes snapped open, and then narrowed into focus. Cleo was on one side of the bed, Harry on the other.

"Time to get up," Harry repeated. "We got visitors."

"We *have* visitors," Abby corrected.

"That's what I said. A big bunch of them. Dad says you gotta come down quick because he needs help."

"Hey. That's enough," Abby told her dog as she gave a little push in the wrong direction and tried vainly to wipe off her wet nose. Her dog hung on the edge of the bed for a minute with her tongue hanging out, panting. Finally, Cleo dropped to the floor—just barely in time, of course, because on the other side Harry scrambled up as fast as he could on top of the bed and kissed her on her nose in exactly the same place that the dog had licked. "Enough! Enough already," Abby called. "What is this?"

"I'm practicing," Harry said. "Daddy told me to practice. Mommy."

"Daddy told you to practice *Mommy*?"

"Yes, he told me to keep practicing to say that because there are some people here who are going to be very mean to Daddy if we don't all say the right words. Come on." Harry reached under the sheet, the only covering that Abby possessed, and snatched at her wrist. He tried to pull her out of the bed but at just that moment Abby realized that somewhere during the course of the night she had lost every little covering that she possessed. She grabbed for the top of the sheet, pulled it up around her neck as high as possible and said to the pair of them, "Come on now, I have to get dressed. I can't go downstairs like this. What's going on?"

"We have lots of visitors," Harry repeated. "People what came on the boat today. Lots of them. They got a meeting going in the dining room and Daddy says, 'Go and get Mommy, right away.'"

"Go and get *Mommy* right away?"

"So I came. You gotta hurry. There's a crowd of 'em."

"Oh, all right," Abby said, "I'm hurrying! Now, you two scoot out of here."

She sat up in her bed, clutching her sheet around her, and smiled as she watched the two of them. Her mismatched pair of knights swaggered out of the door and shut it behind them. Only then did she drop her sheet and stretch. Lord, how good it felt. She ached in every bone, and where every bone had a muscle she ached in that too. A pleasant ache, the sort of ache that she would love to try again, but would not. Perhaps never. Because, she reminded herself, it had to be a one-night stand.

Selby has no intention of getting married again—at least not to me. He'll probably go back to his first wife for the boy's sake. I don't believe I could ever work up to that much love and devotion with any other man, she thought. I have had all the joy, I suppose, that I'll ever get. I might just as well retire to a convent. With that she tumbled out of bed, found herself a pair of pants that were not too dirty and a nice long-sleeved blouse that covered her shoulders. Somehow or other she had accumulated teeth marks on those shoulders.

She slipped her feet into a pair of sandals. Her hair was a mess, as it always was. She took a brush and gave it forty whacks. That didn't seem to impress her hair at all, but it was all she could do for the moment. And then downstairs she went.

Harry had been right—there was a crowd in the dining room. Fifteen or twenty people perhaps, men and women, all standing around like a bunch of wolves baying at Selby Farnsworth. He was trapped in the center of the crowd with a simple smile on his face, daring them to do their worst. And that was just what they were doing. The uproar was louder than a subway ride.

Questions were coming at him from all directions. "What about the farm bill, Congressman?"

"Do you think that you had the right to leave at this critical time in the legislative year?"

"Is it true that you're playing house with a young lady?"

There were a dozen or more ideas popping out here and there, and he answered not one of them—until finally he saw Abby's arrival at the back of the room. He waved her forward to join him. A smile broke through her solemnity, just for a moment. He was so much taller than all the others present that he could signal over their heads. For some reason that was pleasant. But her smile faded when she found Harrelson of the *Gazette* glaring at her.

"Caught you this time," he sneered.

"Did you, now?" she returned in her most gentle voice.

Cleo joined her there, Harry also. With one of them on each side of her Abby made her way gradually through the crowd. It was difficult in the beginning. The people with their backs to her in the rear of the crowd didn't want to lose their position. Finally, they recognized that the answer to their problem was marching across the crowded dining room behind them. Their shouted questions faded. They broke away in front of her and made a little path.

"Well, now, it's about time," Selby said as she came up to him. He picked up the boy, gave him a kiss, patted the dog and then swept up Abby in both his arms and gave her a kiss. The kind that lasted for more than the required thirty seconds. The kind that brought a lot of "oohs" and "ahhs" from the female media people. The kind that had them all clamoring for answers to questions by the time the kiss was over.

When he put Abby down she was thoroughly, totally exhausted. Completely out of breath. Totally out of understanding.

"What in the world is going on?" she whispered to him.

"I'm making up a story," he said. "Stick with me."

"Yeah, sure," she muttered. "The road to hell is paved——"

"We're not in the paving business," he hissed, and gave her a little shake.

"And now, ladies and gentlemen..." Selby announced as loudly as he could. The wolf pack in front of him grew gradually quieter. "Let me present to you my pride and joy. Cleo, our dog, Harry, our son, and Abby, my wife."

An absolute calm fell over the room for as much as a minute. People with tape recorders were fumbling with them to make sure that they were getting it all down accurately. Pencils were scraping across notebook pages. Finally, the question, "You came out to the island for your honeymoon, Congressman?" broke the silence.

"That's Peter Chasen from the *Washington Mirror*, isn't it?"

"Right, that's me."

"Yes, Abby and I came out here to make a family adjustment. It's our honeymoon, Harry's vacation and Cleo's job. Now, as you can see, we're healthy. We're happy. I think we'll go for another two days before we make our way back to the congress of these United States. I have to tell you, not being the meekest of all the representatives in the House, I know that the governing body can get along without us for at least another couple of days. Now, gentlemen, do you have any questions?"

"Is it a coincidence," the *Mirror* reporter interjected, "that you snuck away and married Cicero? Does our editor know?" There was a silence. Everybody had a question, and it popped out on all sides.

"Who's Cicero?"

"The book reviewer on the *Mirror*," Peter Chasen replied, and grinned as he qualified his statement. "The girl with the vitriol pen."

Another buzz of conversation swelled. Abby looked cautiously up at Selby. His smile had disappeared. His gentle hug became a death grip.

"Didn't you review one of the congressman's books?" Peter asked.

Abby ducked her head. If it was going to rain down all over her she didn't want to let it catch her with her mouth open.

"Of course she did," Selby said. "My first one. She taught me a great deal in that little review. There's where we met." He gave his new "wife" a little squeeze. Abby felt as if two of her ribs had broken.

"Where can I get a telephone?" a reporter called.

"Well, now, that, I'm afraid, you'll have to figure out for yourself," Selby said. "We don't have a telephone out here on the island, luckily for us. We don't have a lot of things, just our family and a little loving. So if you want to get the word back to your editors I would suggest that you haul yourselves down to the dock and find the same boat that brought you. There's a telephone at the Woods Hole dock. If you're not in that much of a hurry, then my wife and I invite you to join us in a toast to *long life* and *happiness*."

He made a sweeping gesture with one arm, pointing to the table behind him, where rows of bottles were stacked. Purely by accident, Abby hoped, he managed to give her another jarring. But when he hit her again on the way back she drew a different conclusion.

"How come I had to wait until now to find that out, Cicero?" he muttered as he leaned to kiss her cheek.

"You never asked," she returned angrily. She stabbed at his foot with her sandals, forgetting that she had no high heels to punish him with. "A girl has to make her living somehow or another."

"Serves you right," he added as she groaned at the damage to her own foot. Frustrated, Abby stood, shaking, in the circle of his arms as he kissed her again.

"He turns you on, doesn't he?" one of the women reporters commented as she went by, heading for the drinks table. The crowd surged forward to join her. Selby urged the four of them away from the moving mob.

"Did you hear?" he murmured, chuckling. "They're all jealous of you, wife."

"I'm going to kill you for this," she hissed at him.

"After the reporters leave," he said. "We musn't get our domestic problems into the national papers.

"A little toast, if you would, ladies and gentlemen of the Press," he announced. "Serve yourselves. Glasses are on the table to my left. The bottles are here and I believe that we have enough to offer everyone a drink."

One of the more enterprising young newsmen walked up to the table and picked up one of the bottles. "Cognac," he yelled. "French cognac!"

That caused a few more interested heads to turn toward the table itself. An elderly man picked up another bottle near by. "Holy hell," he roared. "Look at this, will you? French cognac, 1872. Who ever drank liquor like this before?"

There was a mass movement from within the crowd. Everyone jostled around the table, grabbing bottles as if their lives depended on it.

As the crowd passed, Selby gathered his family up in his arms and backed into a corner with them. There was no need to help the reporters; they knew very well how to go about the activity before them.

"Well, how 'bout that?" Harry said.

"Yes," Selby said and his voice was prim and cold. "How about that?"

"What kind of game are you playing, Mr. Farnsworth?" Abby's cold tone matched his face.

"Well," Selby said, "I couldn't think of anything else that would be as effective as that particular story. Could you?"

"Honeymoon? Lovey dovey? Man and wife and dog and boy? Lord, you may have saved your good name, Congressman," she said, "but you have ruined my reputation. What are all my people going to say? Abby Spencer marries Selby Farnsworth? What arrant nonsense. They all know that you're not the marrying kind. My God, it's bad enough to have to put up with all these days of harum-scarum living. But to find out that I'm an unmarried bride at the end of it—that's too much.''

Selby tugged her up under his arm. Although she was a tall girl, she fitted very snugly under his arm. "I really thought, Abby," he said, "that after last night——"

She held up her hand. He was speaking softly so that even little Harry couldn't hear. She stopped him with her eyes. "Last night," she said, "was a one-time thing. Maybe it was even a mistake on my part. Last night was something that I'll never do again."

"Oh, brother!" he said. "A one-night stand?"

"Of course," she said. "Did you think I was going to get a license and go into the business?"

"Well, I don't know what to say," Selby said. "I don't know what to say."

"Whatever you think you might want to say, say it now," Abby told him. "After the crowd leaves there won't be any more discussion. Your son needs his mother, not some stranger. The congress needs a congressman. But I don't need you!"

"What are you," he grumbled, "a Republican?"

Cleo barked. They both looked down. The dog was sitting up by Selby's foot, staring at them both, her tongue hanging out, panting. Harry had shifted over to the other side and now stood next to Abby with his arms up around her waist. "Mommy," he said tentatively. "Momma?"

"You need a *real* mother," she told the boy, and ducked her head away to hide the tears.

It took an hour for the reporters to remember that they were due to report the news. They gradually began to filter out of the house, offering their congratulations to the happy pair, offering their hopes for the future to the two of them, offering a request for a free bottle, nine or ten of them. With all of them, Selby acted with charm, herding them along with his grin. He stood at the door with his arm around Abby as the last few filtered out of the dining room.

The obnoxious Harrelson, now "several sheets to the wind," bustled up to them, carrying a half-empty bottle. He waved the bottle in Selby's face. "You can't fool me with all this," he announced grandly. "I know damn well you're not married. Just playing house, you two. I got it all from your ex-wife!"

"I'll mail you a wedding picture," Selby commented.

"Do that," the reporter said. "This is for the Sunday paper. If I get a wedding picture before Press time I'll kill the story. Otherwise—and don't think I won't include your attempted bribery. Free 1872 cognac. Where do you get your income, Congressman?"

As the door slammed behind the man, Selby dropped his arm from around Abby's shoulders and gave a sigh of exhausted relief. "I'd like to break that man's neck."

"Now then," Abby said. "What's to be done about this?"

"What's to be done about what?" Selby asked innocuously.

"Don't for the Lord's sake tease me any more, Selby," she said. There was a tiredness in her voice, a sense of the end of expectations. "The party's over. There's no more time or place to run. Tomorrow, I guess I'll go home. I suppose you will too. I'm not married. You're not married——"

A little old lady came out of the dining room, one that they hadn't noticed in all the crowd. "You're not married?" she said, looking at Abby.

"Aunt Letty!" Abby said. "What in the world are you doing here?"

"Well, one thing I'm doing here," said her great-aunt, "is trying to settle what's going on in these parts. What do you mean, you're not married? Of course you're married. You've just announced it to the entire world, to the public, to the Press. It'll be known all the way from here to Shanghai in about six hours. Of course you're married!"

Aunt Letitia was as small as Abby was tall. Slightly under five feet, a gray wisp of a woman, marked gently by decades of living, dressed in a double-breasted blue suit and wearing a porkpie hat. No one in Abby's memory had ever called her Amaryllis and only a few got to call her Letty.

"Aunt Letitia," Selby said. "Aha! You're the person who leased me occupation rights on this island, didn't you?"

"I certainly did." There was a mischievous smile on her face. "Served two purposes, and it worked both times. I knew if I could get you both together——"

"Aunt Letitia!" Abby said with all the glacial tones it deserved.

"Hush, child. Children should been seen and not heard. You're married! Your mother bet me fifty dollars it wouldn't work. And his lease money—I can't seem to remember your name, boy."

"Selby," he said. "Selby Farnsworth." He sounded as if he too had an Aunt Letty somewhere in his family tree.

"That lease provided me with enough money for a sure thing down at Hialeah," Aunt Letty crowed. "Here I am, prepared to pay you back." Out of the several pockets of her jacket she began to pull out crumpled fifty-dollar bills—two, three, four at a time, and then by the handful. She straightened them out, gave them all a pat, counted them three times and handed them all to Selby. "And that, Mr. Farnsworth," she said. "That is your name, isn't it—Farnsworth?"

"That's my name," Selby admitted. "And what's all this money?"

"I'm paying you back and breaking the lease," Aunt Letitia said. "Now that we've got you two married we don't need the excuse that I thought my brother left me the island—although he should have. Now, what about a celebration party, so that both our families can enjoy the wedding?"

"Well, this is a surprise," Selby said. "You wouldn't have noticed, perhaps, that Harry and I and Abby have been marooned on this island for nigh on a week now. All because of you."

"All because of me," said Aunt Letitia, her little lips, unmarked by cosmetics, flashing against teeth that looked like pearls. "Everything worked out right. I got to Florida just in time and it was Bimini Babe in the fifth race. Two hundred to one, the odds were. Isn't that grand? And I was holding the only winning ticket. Lovely, lovely, lovely. Now then, Abby, what's all this? Tears on your wedding day?"

"I don't know quite how to describe it," Abby said. "I came to spend a quiet vacation here. My boat got loose and wandered off. Selby and his boy showed up. They didn't have a boat. It all got to be very, very confusing. And today the news people ganged up on us and Selby had to think up some kind of story. You know, the papers are full of congressional indiscretions lately. And so he just made up a story off the top of his head, and said we were married. And we aren't!"

"I find that very hard to believe," Aunt Letitia commented. "That kiss you were showing off up front certainly looked married—very recently married, of course.

Are you telling me that's the first time you ever kissed my great-niece, Mr. Farnsworth?''

The congressman from Ohio had suddenly found that his shirt collar was too tight. He ran a finger up between the buttons, and the top one popped off.

"Well, Mr. Farnsworth?"

"I—perhaps we did kiss—a time or two," he managed to get out.

"And perhaps you might have gone a step or two further?"

"Don't play Inquisition on him," Abby said tiredly. "He's not responsible for everything we might have done."

"So perhaps you could tell me, girl." Her aunt's interrogation had intensified. Almost any minute Abby expected her to pull out a whip for emphasis.

"Tell you what?" Too tired, too confused to dodge the shrapnel, Abby stood there, rocking back and forth on her heels.

"When my niece left home a week ago," Aunt Letitia said, choosing her words carefully in front of the child, "she was a caring Sunday school teacher. Is she now?"

Abby's chin drooped. All her chickens had come home to roost on the same day. "Perhaps not," she said. Selby's arm came around her shoulders, lending a little courage.

"Perhaps won't do," Aunt Letitia snapped. "It's one way or the other. Perhaps won't do. Do you expect that you're half pregnant——?"

"No, Miss Spencer," Selby interrupted. "No chance. I took particular care."

"The only guarantee I ever heard of is abstinence, Mr. Farnsworth." Aunt Letitia stopped long enough to think. "Would you, young man, get me a glass of water?"

Harry looked up at his father, who nodded agreement. The boy shook his head in disgust. "Come on, Cleo," the child said. "I know most of the words. I'll explain it to you in the kitchen." With which he and the dog walked out.

Aunt Letitia watched as the pair left the room. "Smart young man," she commented. "He'd make a fine stepson. Now then, you two. If you're *not* married you ought to be. And it's not too late to take care of that."

Oh, yes, it is, Abby told herself. Selby doesn't *want* to be married. Not to me, at least. But he's too proud to say so. I'm not going to stand here and watch him railroaded into it. "No," she said firmly. "There's no need for a marriage, and we're not going to have you talk us into it. Just because we've exchanged a kiss or two——"

"Hah!" her aunt interrupted.

"Well, whatever we did, I'm not going to marry him!"

She turned her back on the pair of them, and missed the glance they exchanged.

"In that case," Aunt Letitia said, "you've blown his alibi wide-open. If that man from the *Gazette* doesn't get his wedding pictures in the mail he's going to make a crusade out of all this. I don't mind seeing Farnsworth in the soup, but I fear for his son—Harry? Is that the boy's name? I fear for Harry."

Abby whirled around, the tears in her eyes plainly visible. "I am *not* going to marry him," she shouted. "Not even for Harry!"

"And what do you say, Mr. Farnsworth?"

"I admit that Harry and I will have a great deal of difficulty," he said, "but I can't *make* her marry me. So I suppose I might just as well go back to Washington tomorrow and face the music."

See, there, Abby told herself, I've given him the perfect excuse not to marry me, and he's taking it!

"I almost never deal in subterfuge," Aunt Letitia said thoughtfully. She ignored the "hmph" that Abby failed to suppress. "But perhaps if we sustain this—fiction— for a time things might possibly blow over."

"The lie, you mean," Abby commented. Both Selby and her aunt stared at her as if she had brought in worms for lunch.

"The fiction," Aunt Letitia repeated. "I have some good friends in Hyannis—a touring company that's doing *The Marriage Game* for the next week. I could probably get some of them to come over tomorrow, and bring a photographer as well. We could stage a fake marriage in the living room, make plenty of photos, and send them to that Harrelson man. My friends are professionals. Believe me, you wouldn't know the difference from the real. Would that satisfy? Mr. Farnsworth?"

"Yes," he said quickly. "It would certainly flesh out the story. And then if I tell the editor of the *Gazette* that his man was here and got himself totally drunk on *our* cognac I think that would take care of everything."

"Abby?"

"It would still be a lie," Abby murmured. "God, I hate it. All the lies we've stacked up against us. But—I don't care! If that's what you both want, I'll go through with it! Damn you all. I hope my mother never finds out!"

The tears broke free, and came running down her cheeks. She clenched her fists, glared at the pair of them, and looked for the stairs through the curtain of rain. "But when all the plotting is done I won't be married to Selby, and I don't intend to be married to Selby. If he were the only man left in the world I might consider it, but not otherwise." She darted up the stairs, slammed the door of her room behind her, and fell onto the bed, sobbing. She wept at twenty-six tears to the inch. It seemed as if the house might sink with the weeping.

Harry and the dog came back from the kitchen at the same moment. "I brought your water," Harry announced.

"Ugh," Aunt Letitia snorted. "Put it on the side table there. I never drink the stuff. Mr. Farnsworth, is there any more of that cognac left?"

"Your brother left a treasure," he said. "There are a great many bottles left. Follow me."

A moment or two later, in the kitchen, over strong drink, Selby offered a toast. "I pray I might learn not to talk with my mouth open, Aunt Letitia."

"Don't you Aunt Letitia me," she said. "I am Miss Spencer to you. Miss Spencer, have you got that?"

"Yes, I've got that," Selby said, "but I don't know what I'm going to do with it. So Abby's brokenhearted, and I don't blame her. Still——"

"Still, you wouldn't want to marry her," Aunt Letitia said.

"I'm a damn fool," the congressman admitted. "Of course I want to marry her. I need her, Harry needs her and, dear God, we all need the dog. But what's to be done, Miss Spencer?"

A brilliant smile broke out on her face. "So you've finally seen the light, have you, son? You may call me Aunt Letty. And now I'll tell you what we're going to do. Is there more of this cognac available?"

At seven-thirty that evening, Abby woke from her tear-stained nap, and looked moodily out of the window. Yesterday's storm had long since departed. From down the hall she could hear Harry and his father talking. Her eyelids were stiff from the weeping. She slipped into her bathrobe, snatched up a bath towel, and started down the hall. The pair of them came to Selby's door as she approached. She stopped without invitation.

Harry came out to her, offering a hug without words. Selby tagged along. Abby appreciated the warmth of his hug. It surely wouldn't be cheating if she stopped for a moment and rested her head on his shoulder. It was such a convenient shoulder—the kind a girl might want to keep around the house for use from time to time.

"I—thought I would take a shower," she offered. "Where's my aunt?"

"Aunt Letty kept her own boat and boatman at the wharf," Selby said. "She's gone off to the mainland to meet some friends."

"Aunt Letty?" Abby marveled at that. Only the elder generation of her family were entitled to use that name.

"She asked me to call her that," Selby said. He was pursing his lips. From experience Abby recognized that he was walking carefully, word-wise. Butter wouldn't melt in his mouth!

She worked her way out of Harry's hug, and took one step in the direction of the bathroom when a telephone rang.

"Excuse me," Selby said as he walked over to his wardrobe and took down a cellular phone. "I was expecting this call from Washington." Abby came into the room behind him and stood with both hands on her hips, her face flushed. He put the phone down.

"Not the call I expected," he said. "Wrong number. I gave them the right one. Why is your face so red?"

"Another lie," she snarled, gesturing toward the telephone. "You had that here all the time, and never said a word about it!"

Selby grinned at her. "I am, of course, the only one on this island who ever concealed something like that, lied about it, so to speak?"

"Of course," she said. "I wouldn't——"

And at that moment another telephone started ringing, up the hall.

"Here, let me help you," Selby said. He vaulted off the bed, took Abby's elbow in one of his huge hands, and started to tow her up the corridor toward her own room. The telephone continued to ring.

"I'll get it," Abby said, sighing.

"No need to," Selby insisted jovially. "Now let me see? In the closet? Up on the shelf?" He found the telephone almost as if he knew where to look. After a moment's exchange he handed the instrument over to Abby. "Here, it's for you. Somebody in Washington wants to talk to Cicero."

Her face turned as red as it ever could. She handed the telephone back to him. "Tell them she's not home," she said, and then ran for the bathroom. Behind her she heard his voice echoing with laughter.

"One for me, one for you," he called. She slammed the bathroom door behind her to shut off the laughter. When it still echoed in her ears she turned on both the hot and cold water at the same time, and stood close to the tub. The steam came up into her eyes. She breathed it in deeply, then stepped out of her robe. The full-length mirror standing on the wall opposite her began to fog over. Daydreaming, Abby walked over to it and wrote "One for me" in the fog. And then, after some hesitation, on the far side, "One for him."

Through the interstices of the letters she could see herself. Abby Spencer was not the type of woman who looked often at her entire body. Now it seemed the thing to do. It was what *he* had looked at on the previous night. And with some enjoyment, too. And she wondered why.

He had said something about her hair. She tugged at the bobby pins and let the whole mass of it fall down over her shoulders. Not as long as once it had been, but down to mid-waist, at that. Wet now, it gleamed in the reflected light.

Those teeth marks on her shoulders. Nibbling there, he said, because he'd break a tooth on her earrings! With a wicked grin she brought her hair forward to cover shoulders and breasts, then, after another moment of reflection, took the studs out of her pierced ears. "Possibly too late," she murmured to her reflection. "But who knows? Maybe some other man would want to nibble on my ears—as improbable as that might seem. Or, even more improbable, maybe Selby would like to have just one more bite? I wonder if his family came from Transylvania?"

The steam had wiped out the letters on the mirror, and canceled her show. But she knew the rest. Firm, rotund breasts that he had caressed, narrowing down to a tiny waist that he could almost encircle between his two hands; the wild swelling of her hips, where he had rested his weight.

And everything I am will always remind me of him, she told herself fiercely. To stop the tears from coming she turned and leaped into the tub, where the water was just a tad too cold for her tastes. She squealed.

The bathroom door rattled. "Is something wrong?" Selby called from outside.

"No," she yelled. "The water's just a little too—cold."

"Want me to come in and heat it up?"

"No!" It wasn't the right answer, but it was the *right* answer.

"Spoilsport," he called back, cheerfully. "Harry's in bed, waiting for you to come tell him a story."

Any appeal to good works always brought a response from Abigail Spencer. She ducked her head in the water, used the facecloth to scrub her neck, and came up out of the water like a dolphin in play. Water dripped in all directions. Abby paused until the flood subsided and began to drain off. The doorknob rattled in reminder.

"I'm coming," she yelled as she wrapped the huge bath towel around herself, and began the seesaw motion that dried off her back and other places. Her hair had earned a wrap-up in a smaller towel. Her feet were still wet as she shoved them into her sandals. The doorknob rattled again as she slipped into her robe. It stuck in places not thoroughly dried, but she dared not wait a moment longer. Laughing, she turned the knob and opened the door.

"You mean that it wasn't locked?" he asked in astonishment.

"It wasn't locked," she agreed as he looked her over.

"What a fool I've been," he said. He reached out in her direction. She walked into the curve of his arms.

"I'm the one who's been the fool," she told him. "We've both been holding things back from each other, and I want to apologize."

"No need for either of us to apologize," he returned. "We didn't know each other at the beginning of the game——"

"And I'm truly sorry that the game is over," she interrupted him. He opened his mouth to say something more. She stretched upward and closed his lips with a kiss.

"But——" he managed to say before she placed a hand over his mouth.

"But the game is over and Harry is waiting," she said. Luckily he could not hear her heart skip a beat.

"Come on, you guys," Harry yelled.

Selby gathered her up in his arms and carried her out of the bathroom. In the doing the towel around her head fell by the wayside and he left it there on the floor. His hands were busy, but he thrust his face into the mass of her hair and inhaled. "I've never known a woman to smell so sweet."

"Hurry up or I'll be asleep before you get here," his son complained.

"Somehow I doubt that very much," Abby responded as Selby stretched her out on the bed beside the child.

"This story," Abby said, "is about Ruprecht von Popodopolis, the great German warrior who blew up the powder tower of Heidelberg Castle by mistake, while protecting it from the Sun King, Louis of France."

It was an exciting story, but it had been a long day for Harry, and the boy was gone within ten minutes.

"I wish I had that skill," Selby whispered as he escorted Abby out into the corridor. With an arm around her, he turned them both north, in the direction of her room. She stopped him.

"No," she said. "Not again." She touched his face with her hand, absorbing the toughness of his skin, the prickle of his coming beard.

"But how do I find out what happened to Ruprecht?"

"Write to the Popodopolis library," she suggested. "That's at 123 Fourth Street, Long Branch, New Jersey."

"You have a hard heart." He sighed.

"Yes," she agreed. She went up on her toes for an instant, and kissed his cheek. He tried to hold her, but she oozed out of his hands like mercury, and was gone before he could complain.

"The wedding's tomorrow morning," he called after her. It seemed, in the semidarkness, that she waved acknowledgement. Shaking his head dolefully, Selby Farnsworth went back to his own bed, and tossed and turned all night.

CHAPTER NINE

MISCELLANEOUS noises brought Abby downstairs on the day of the ceremony. Her body ached with unknown pleasures, but her mind was deep in the blues. Everything he had said and everything he had done was locked into her mind. I'll get your mother back. Wasn't that what he had told the boy? Leaving to Abby all the pains and sorrows, without a chance for the completion of her dreams. All that was left was this wedding charade.

The wedding party had already arrived. It consisted of her aunt Letty, a gentleman who introduced himself as the Reverend Mr. Playfair, a lady who introduced herself as Mrs. Playfair, and several young people who merely said they had come along for the ride. Abby hadn't known just what to do about this so-called "wedding," so she'd dressed in her typical uniform—pants, blouse and a pair of sandals. Her aunt caught her just at the foot of the stairs and ushered her into the living room, closing the door behind her.

"This is for you," she said as she presented a package of some considerable size.

Abby approached it cautiously. She knew the old routine about Greeks bearing gifts and her aunt had certainly been acting like an Athenian during this whole incident. So she unfolded the little ties, opened the whole thing up and found a dress—a pure white knee-length dress, a confection of lace and satin and gold which was as beautiful as one could ask for in a dress.

"Put it on," Aunt Letty commanded.

"But—it's white," Abby said.

"So don't worry about that," her aunt suggested. "Nobody pays any attention to colors these days. Besides, it's only *almost* white. Slip it on, there's a good girl."

Abby fought for a minute. She no longer considered herself to be very girlish, and, as for being a "good" girl, her Calvinist conscience told her that Abigail Spencer was a very long way from that. But Aunt Letty was adamant, and with that kind of encouragement Abby put the dress on. It fitted perfectly. She made mention of that to her aunt, who said, "You didn't expect I'd come all the way from Washington and not bring your measurements, did you?"

Abby shrugged her shoulders. There was no knowing what was going on with the eldest generation of the Spencer family. The two of them walked out of the living room and down the hall to the dining room. A tasteful recreation of a chapel had already been made—a couple of tables moved, a podium set up, flowers of considerable proportions masked while they accentuated—and the Reverend Jonathan Playfair. He was a tall man of medium years, whose frame seemed to bend slightly at the neck. A fringe of white hair surrounded his bald pate. He was dressed in clerical robes and was waiting with a smile.

"Are we ready?" he said.

"I'm not," the cameraman said from the corner. "Give me another minute."

"It isn't his pictures he's worried about," Selby said. "He's got his hands on the cognac."

There was a general laughter and the party managed to sort themselves out.

"Abby, you stand here. Selby, you stand there." Aunt Letty was being the producer for the entire occasion, and perhaps the director too. Abby stood there yearning. Her hand was resting lightly on Selby's arm and the Reverend Mr. Playfair was opening some books, making some statements, all of which went completely over Abby's head. There were pauses for responses. Selby nudged her.

"I do," he said under his breath.

"I do," Abby contributed meekly.

Another space, some more words, a prayer and then the fatal words. "And now, by the power invested in me by the Commonwealth of Massachusetts, I pronounce you man and wife. You may kiss the bride."

So far, Abby had contributed nothing. She had been like a large wax doll standing in the proper position, moving at the appropriate times, speaking when called upon, and now Selby kissed her. It was not, perhaps, the best kiss, nor the kiss of which he was most capable, but it was a kiss that inflamed and partially melted wax dolls. She accepted it and calmed down and nestled in his arms, while all around them gathered the people who had come as spectators. Each of them had a glass of cognac in hand. The supply seemed inexhaustible.

"I wondered why they came," Selby said. "Now I see. This is really a treasure." Flash bulbs stung his eyes and caused him to blink.

"That may be," Abby said, "but at the rate we're going there won't be any of it for our first anniversary."

"And now are you all married up?" Harry interjected.

"Well, I guess we're as married as we're going to get," Abby said cautiously. "What is it?"

"Well, are you my mommy now?"

"For the time being," Abby answered gravely, "let's say I am. Then what?"

"Then I gets to kiss you too," said Harry. He tried his best to climb up her white-clad frame to reach her mouth. When he was obviously not going to make it Selby leaned down, snatched him up in his arms and lifted him up to the level of Abby's chin. The little boy kissed her with enthusiasm and then squealed to be put down.

"You're not interested in kissing any more?" Abby asked.

"Oh, that's all right for girls," Harry said, "and I don't mind for a wedding or, you know, something special, but once is enough, huh?" With that, he ran off to the kitchen and Cleo followed him away.

"There's soda in the kitchen," Selby said. "And now for this crowd."

"And now for this crowd?"

"Yes, somehow or other we have to get rid of them now that we've got them here."

"I don't think so," Abby said. "Aunt Letty will take care of that. If you'll excuse me?"

"I will for a few minutes but don't be gone too long," Selby said. "Where are you going?"

"Oh, I think I'll go upstairs and change out of this beautiful dress," Abby said. "I think I need something more commonplace, something more substantial. You'll excuse me?"

"For a time," Selby called after her.

She made her way up the stairs and quietly into her room. She stripped herself out of the dress and got back into her pants and blouse. She added a weatherproof coat to her ensemble. The weather looked good outside but one could never tell on this side of the Cape. During the previous night, while Aunt Letty had been planning, Abby had done some scheming of her own. She left everything else behind her. She crept down the stairs, managed to get out the front door without anyone seeing her, and walked down the hill toward the dock, leaving all the sights and sounds of conviviality behind her. And why not? she asked herself. There was a bitter taste in her mouth. They had their wedding. Pictures were taken. Oaths were exchanged. All lies, and now Abby Spencer was going home.

There was a boat waiting for her at the dock. She had arranged for it to come the night before. She patted the saluting cannon as she went by, smiling as she remembered the cannonball's lot. She walked down to the end of the pier and climbed down the ladder into the boat. It was powered by an outboard Evinrude, a power source she was quite familiar with. She cast off the lines, primed the engine, pulled the starter and the motor roared immediately. She was about two hundred yards away from the island when a thought struck her. Everything she wanted was behind her, cast off, to be forgotten. She moaned. There was a stab of pain in her stomach. But there could be no turning back. The boat rushed off across the sound and she left it tied up at the dock at Woods Hole. Her car was waiting for her in the adjacent parking lot. She walked over to it and struggled to unlock the door. The vehicle had stood there waiting patiently for her ever since the beginning of this adventure. It started without trouble, and in a moment she was on her way toward Route 195.

The island had almost disappeared. Fog was moving in, a little rain was threatening too. Abby stopped for just a moment at the farthest point from which she could see the island. She dabbed at her eyes with her handkerchief and then drove off toward Virginia and the old family farm house just south of Manassas Junction.

"So this is where you're hiding, Abby," her mother said as she came into the girl's room. Abby was sitting on the floor in a yoga position, elbows on her knees, fists holding her chin up, staring at the wall. Her mother walked over to her and tapped her on the head. "Are you alive?"

"Oh, Mom," she said, sighing, "what's the trouble?"

Her mother walked back over to the only chair in the bedroom. It was a surprising thing to see that Abby was tall, her brothers were taller, her father was taller than they and her mother was five feet three. Still as well formed as she had been at her own wedding, Mrs. Spencer sat down in the rocking chair, brushed her gray hair out of her eyes, and folded her hands.

"What's the trouble?" she echoed. "Are you going to tell me about it? You're sitting on the floor here for the past five days. Your idiot dog is downstairs sitting by the front door as if she's waiting for somebody. Is that what you're up to? Are you both waiting for somebody?"

"Momma," Abby said, "I've done a terrible thing."

"Well, it happens to all of us. Do you want to tell me about it?"

"I—er—I don't think so," Abby said. "I need to think."

"It has something to do with the wedding?"

Abby's head snapped up. "You know about the wedding?"

Her mother chuckled. "Surely you don't think that your great-aunt could think up that much trouble all by herself? I claim a half interest in the disaster." The jollity disappeared from her voice. "I'm sorry, love. It seemed to be such a good idea at the time. Can you see it in your heart to forgive a meddling mother?"

Abby waved the protestation off with a vague hand movement. "Don't be concerned, Mom. For a minute there *I* thought it might be a terrific idea."

"But?"

"But he has this little boy, Harry. A darlin' of a lad, who wants his mother. Selby divorced the woman some years ago, but, for the boy's sake——"

"He might try to get together with his former wife?" her mother interrupted. "I am truly sorry, love. I shall never meddle again."

"Don't be so hard on yourself, Mom. I'll get over it. There's nothing irredeemably lost." No, there certainly isn't, she told herself. Only my heart. And something more, her conscience told her. But that's not terribly important, Abby declared, and knew it was a terrible lie.

"And you're not going to work?"

"No. I—er—quit the job. They wanted me to do a hatchet job on Selby, and I thought that was so bad that I quit the job and told the editor he could stuff it right Oh, Lord, Mom, what words I used. You would have been so embarrassed for me."

"I've known a word or two in my day," her mother said. "It would have hurt, you know." Having lost the thread of the conversation, Abby stared. "Stuffing it," her mother teased. "Very painful.

"You've really had a strange, strange autumn," her mother continued. "You went out of here cheerful and bright with a load of books to review and a good future in hand. And you've come back dragging your heels. Don't you have any plans at all? Your father is waiting for me to tell him whether to file suit; your brothers want the man's address. They'd all like to get together and punch his ticket. What *is* his name?''

''Selby. Selby Farnsworth. And you can tell them all to keep their hands off. If they, any of them, lay a finger on Selby, I'll——''

''As you say,'' her mother chuckled. ''You don't care for the man at all. I'll pass the word.''

She turned to leave the room, and stopped. ''I forgot. You have a letter in the mail this morning.'' She dropped the letter in Abby's lap, patted the bent head of her only daughter and walked out.

Bother, Abby thought, as she looked down at the envelope in her lap. I'd almost forgotten what a letter's like. She picked it up carefully and turned it around in various directions until she could read the address and name of the sender. Immediately, all her senses came to attention.

The letter was addressed to Mr. and Mrs. Selby Farnsworth at a house address in Falls Church. The original address was crossed out in pencil, and a notation added, ''Try P.O. Box 92 RFD#3, Manassas Junction.'' Up in the corner, she saw something she had never expected to see—the writer's return address was the Church of the Holy Trinity, Rev. Jonathan W. Playfair, Hyannis, Massachusetts. For just a moment Abby sat there and looked. Suddenly, all her nerves began to shiver. The Reverend Mr. Playfair, Church of the Holy Trinity. An actor? Huh!

Fumbling because her hands were out of control, as well as her mind, Abby ripped the corner off the envelope and pulled out the double sheet enclosed. It was a congratulatory letter.

''I try as soon as possible after every wedding ceremony,'' the minister wrote, ''to congratulate the people whom I have joined together in God's name and to wish them well. So, for the both of you, although I am a little behind the times, may I take this opportunity to congratulate you and wish you many years of happiness? With God's devotion, Jon W. Playfair, Vicar, Holy Trinity Church, Hyannis.''

Good Lord, Abby said to herself, her fingers were trembling so hard that the second enclosure was crackling back and forth in her hands and she was missing the words. The words that she needed to see were there in black and white—wedding certificate—the Reverend Mr. Playfair—the Church of the Holy Trinity—congratulations—marriage—God bless. And on the envelope—unknown at this address! The monster!

"I'll 'unknown' him," Abby growled. She redoubled her effort to control her body, which was reacting to two different commands. It was all real! Damn the man!

Her mother, downstairs, heard the clatter as Abby jumped to her feet, ravaged her wardrobe, and snatched out a few mismatched items of clothing. She added a sweater, because of the coolness of the day, and came clattering down the stairs with the marriage lines in her hand and murder in her eyes. "It was real," she muttered to her mother as she swept by. "Till death us do part. He's going to find that death and parting are not all that far apart!"

"Going out?" her mother asked as she ducked out of the line of fire.

"Going out," Abby said grimly. "Falls Church, where's that?"

"Why, straight up near Washington," her mother said. "Up there in the upper crust, of course. Are you going to Falls Church?"

"Yes, I'm going to Falls Church."

"What—who?"

"I know a little boy up there," Abby said. "I know a wonderful little boy who needs a mother. I'm going to kill his father! The child would be better off an orphan!"

"Why don't you just volunteer to be the child's mother?"

"Well, I——" Abby had to stop to laugh. "I guess I have to say that I was volunteered. By dear Aunt Letty, by the way. I'll be back some time. Goodbye, Mom." And she rushed out the door.

Not escaping her attention, of course, was Cleo, who had been hugging that door for the last several days. Now that it was opened, with Abby in full pursuit of something, Cleo dashed through the narrow opening and joined up with the hunt.

When they got to the car door, Cleo looked up appealingly. "Yes," Abby said, "you're right. You and I? Huh? You and me? Us! Come on, pooch."

Moments later she was zooming up the highway straight for the heart of Washington. Luckily there were no policemen on the road that afternoon, or she might have arrived hours or even days too late. The old Volkswagen was able to spring up a storm and she sprung it. She found Falls Church by zooming along Route 495 and watching the signs, but hunting down Deborah Drive, a tiny cul-de-sac in the middle of the subdivision called Donna Lee Gardens, required more good luck than common sense. And finding the specific house without knowing the number required the support of angels.

Well, dogs, to be specific. She slowed to a crawl, opened the left back window just an inch or two, and convinced Cleo to go into her "hunting dog" trance. All the way from Waldorf Lane to Arthur Drive they cruised. Cleo whined a couple of times, but only that.

"You've got to do better," Abby coaxed as she made a full circle at the junction of Arthur Drive and started back, cruising slowly along the other side of Deborah Drive. As they approached the junction of Woodley and Deborah the old dog came up off her haunches. And no more than two houses along on the other side of that crossing Cleo began to bay and jump. The car door rattled. Abby pulled to a stop.

The house was dead still. It looked a great deal like its neighbors, but Cleo was in full cry, up the path and to the front door, where she bayed and jumped until someone came to the door.

"She doesn't bite," Abby said to the woman who refused, sensibly, to open the screen door. "She's my dog," Abby called. "I'm—does Selby live here?"

"I don't know if I should say," the tall dark woman said. "Who might you be?"

"Well," said Abby, waving her letter in her ungloved hand, "I might be a lot of things, but what I appear to be just at this moment is Mrs. Selby Farnsworth."

"Lord almighty," the woman said. "Come you in, come in. I'm Mrs. Premm."

Abby walked into a well-furnished living room. "Heel," she commanded her dog, and to her surprise the dog responded. "Harry?" Abby asked. "Is Harry——?"

"Never seen anything like it," Mrs. Premm interrupted. "Both of them. The mister came back acting as if he had a set of permanent boils. And the boy—he's got the dismals real bad. Won't eat, doesn't sleep, won't go to school. I just don't know what to make of things."

"Is Selby——?"

"At the Capitol, my dear. Morning, noon and night he's down at the Capitol. Comes home every night late, and then him and Harry, they sit together on the couch and don't say a word."

Abby shook her head. We *three* have the dismals, she thought. But before she could explore the idea Cleo reached the end of her patience and dashed up the stairs. From above them there came a shout of glee. Cleo barked madly.

"That sounds as if it's a partial solution," Mrs. Premm said, smiling. "Now, let me get you a cup of coffee, and you can sit and tell me all about it. I'm the housekeeper, the cook, the nanny—and everything else you can think of. Come in. Come in. I've heard a lot about you."

"Oh, have you really?" said Abby, flabbergasted. "I can't imagine what it was. Nothing good, I expect."

"Don't run yourself down, my dear. As far as I can tell, from listening to Harry and his father, you are related to the angels."

"You're close," Abby replied. "Selby wants to murder me, I think. He's planning to set me among the angels." She meant to say more, but there was an explosion of noise from above.

Coming down the stairs were one dog and one boy, hanging on to each other as if their lives depended on it. When they got to the bottom stair Harry stopped, patted Cleo's head and looked across the living room to where Abby was standing. He squinted for a minute against the specks of light coming through the window curtains.

"Abby?" he said tentatively. And then, more sure of himself, "Momma!" With that, he dashed across the room and jumped up into Abby's arms.

"Momma, indeed," Abby said as she cuddled the warm, sweet head against her. "Mommy, indeed. I guess that you've gotten yourself a bargain-basement mother, Harry. At least, that's what this letter says. When your dad comes home for lunch——"

"He never comes home for lunch," Harry said. "He don't never seem to be home at all."

Abby nodded her head. One more nail in Selby Farnsworth's coffin. A very ornate funeral it was going to be.

"You're not mad at me any more?" the boy asked. Cleo was licking his nose.

"I never was angry with *you*," Abby said.

"But—but you're angry with my dad?"

"As mad as can be," Abby said solemnly. "I'm looking for your dad, and when I find him—I don't really know what I'm going to do, but it'll be *something*. You can bet on that!" Abby lifted her arm to look at her wristwatch. Ten-thirty. "Never comes home for lunch?" she asked.

"Never. It never used to be like this either," said the housekeeper. "Always used to be a casual man. Today he's all fierce, all temper. Every time he smiles since he's come home I think maybe his face is going to crack."

"I'm going to help him crack it," Abby announced.

"Poor Daddy," Harry said, but there was a gleam in his eye.

The doorbell rang. All the conversations stopped; all the smiles disappeared. Mrs. Premm, looking as if she expected trouble, went to the door and opened it.

"Well, it's about time." A tall blond woman was on the step. A thin whippet of a man accompanied her. They brushed by the housekeeper.

"No," Harry yelled as he tried to hide behind Abby.

"That's the boy, Alfred," the woman said. "Grab him and we'll be on our way."

"Just a darn minute," Abby said. "Mr. Farnsworth isn't home at the moment——"

"I know that," the woman said. "That's why we've come at this time. Grab the boy, Alfred."

Alfred, who looked to be about five feet six and a featherweight, started for Harry, but Abby stepped between them. Trouble, she told herself. Just the kind of trouble I need. Maybe I can work off my enthusiasm here. Maybe I won't have to beat up on Selby?

"Let me restate the problem," Abby said in her best Sunday school voice. "Selby is not here. You are not going to take Harry anyplace without Selby's permission."

"I happen to be the boy's mother," the woman said. "Grab him, Alfred!"

Alfred tried his best. He was wearing a very fashionable and very expensive blue suit jacket. Abby took the lapels in both hands and lifted him to his tiptoes. He made a couple of inarticulate noises, and tried to kick a time or two.

"Alfred," Abby said. "Listen carefully. I'm going to set you down on the floor and count to five. If you're not out the door by the time I reach five, I'm going to stomp all over you. Got it?"

Alfred's head bobbed. It might well have been an affirmative. Abby was willing to give it a chance. She lowered him to where his toes touched the floor, turned him around to point at the door, and gave him a little shove. Mrs. Premm, her face lit with a broad smile, opened the door. Alfred went through it pumping at five miles an hour. By the time Abby counted up to three he was gone.

"Now then." Abby turned her attention to the woman. A suicide blonde. The roots of her hair gave her away. A pancake face. Somewhere under there was probably a layer of skin, but one would be guessing. "Just who might you be, lady?"

"I am the boy's mother," the woman said. "When we were divorced the court awarded custody to me, but I couldn't afford to keep him. But now that Alfred and I are married and have a settled home I intend to have my son with me. I will, of course, require higher alimony payments. And just who are you?"

Abby's mind, which had been working on "low" for weeks, jumped into high gear. Selby's former wife had kept him in the poorhouse because of her alimony payments. But when a woman remarried all bets were off!

"You don't have a snowball's chance in hell, either for getting Harry or getting more alimony," Abby announced. "Selby has already established a settled home for Harry. As for me, I'm the latest Mrs. Farnsworth. You might take your problem up with the courts, but I'm sure if you do you'll find your alimony payments are permanently canceled."

"Remarried? I don't believe it. He would never do that. Never. I want my son." She took another step or two in Harry's direction. The boy squirmed behind her.

"Don't let her, Abby."

"Never a chance," Abby assured him. "You're *my* son now."

The blonde froze in position. She flicked a quick glance over her shoulder. Alfred was already in the driver's seat of their car. She licked her lips. "I want my son," she snarled.

Abby moved slowly in her direction. The blonde was about five feet eight. Abby topped her by a good two inches. "Let me make you an offer you can't refuse," Abby said soothingly. "How would you like a nice punch in the mouth?" She lifted her right hand, displaying a tightly folded fist. "Or maybe two?"

"I——" The blonde conceded defeat. Still spitting and snarling, she backed out the door. As soon as it closed behind her Cleo rushed up and started to bark her head off.

"Nice dog," Abby muttered. "Nice dog. Good guard dog!"

Harry came out from behind her. He looked as if he was just beginning to breathe. "Was you really gonna hit her?"

"Who knows?" Abby replied. "I have a very bad temper."

"I'll remember," Harry said. "I'll remember—Mommy."

"And now I've got to move. I need to catch your father, Harry."

"Are you gonna punch him too?" The boy was smiling, as if it might be a sight to see.

"A man his size? I'm not *that* crazy. You stay here with Mrs. Premm and Cleo."

"Driving in?" the housekeeper asked pleasantly.

Abby gave her a quick look. "Are you planning to call and warn him?"

"Not me. I raised that boy from a pup. He deserves everything you can provide. No, I only wanted to say it's almost impossible to find a parking place in the Capitol area. As it happens, Mr. Farnsworth took his second car with him today. The other one is parked out back. It has congressional plates."

"Aha." Abby reached out for the keys the housekeeper was offering. Congressional plates were not exactly the be-all that once they were. Police had no second thoughts about ticketing a congressman's car parked illegally. But they still hesitated to tow one such away to the police compound, and the ticket itself often received more courteous treatment than a plain citizen got. "Cleo, you stay here with Harry," she offered. The dog woofed agreeably and sat down on the boy's foot. "Harry, you take care of Cleo. Now I'm going to go say a word or two to your father."

And with that Abby dashed out, forgetting to close the front door, letting the cool of autumn into the house.

CHAPTER TEN

WASHINGTON CITY had changed a great deal since Pierre L'Enfant did the major design work, way back when. Now it had more marble than wood, more prejudices than people—although there were always enough people to go around—and more tourists than anyone knew what to do with.

All these various kinds of people drove various kinds of cars. Sometimes, on bad days, all those people and all those cars came to a disagreement, at which time all the streets in Washington would become gridlocked, and they all turned into parking lots. Which upset the police force mightily.

Abby came across the river into the city on the Arlington Memorial Bridge, one fly speck among a thousand others. Noontime was perhaps not the best time to drive around the city, but who could choose? At the Lincoln Memorial circle she edged over onto Independence Avenue, proceeded in stately fashion along the Mall and by the Reflecting Pool, and turned left on First Street.

The large stately Capitol building stood in all its glory on her left hand. The Capitol building, of course, ran north and south, but faced east. Or, if your organization rated only a small ceremony *behind* the building, it faced west.

But, no matter which way it faced, the Capitol police were facing in *all* directions at the moment. Dispirited, Abby noticed that some of the reserved spaces around

177

the Library of Congress were empty. She hardly delayed
a moment before filling one of them—the one marked
"Director."

"What the hey?" she reasoned aloud as she locked
the car door. "If a congressman can't park at the
Congressional Library, who can?" So, whistling, occasionally looking back, she made her way across the
open spaces toward the Capitol. Although she was
walking quickly, by the time she made it to the other
side of First Street a policewoman was already ticketing
the car. Abby shrugged her shoulders. Just one more
little problem for Selby to solve, she told herself. She
squared her shoulders and marched smartly north to the
massive steps, and into the shade of the east portico.

There was a guard at the main entrance, who demanded identification. Ever since an underground group
of Puerto Rican Independencia had made it into the
gallery and taken a few potshots at legislators, everything was guarded.

"I'm Mrs. Farnsworth," she told the man.

"I'm happy for you," he responded pleasantly. "You
still need some identification."

Frustrated, almost in tears, Abby fumbled with her
bag. It slipped off her shoulder, and bits and pieces cas-
caded all over the marble steps. When traffic was slow,
and no supervisors were watching, even Capitol guards
could be nice to a pretty girl—especially if she was crying.
He bent down quickly and managed to gather all the
little odds and ends together. The last item he found was
her card case. When he held it up all the several plastic
sections unfolded, displaying her multitude of cards and
licenses and permits.

"Ah. Here's the one." He had gone down to the end
of the file, to where her identity card from the *Mirror*

was located. True, it was no longer valid since she just didn't work there any more, but the guard was so sure of its value that he waved her through with a cheery smile. She did her best to return the smile as she crammed everything back into her purse.

Luck was with her. Just inside the hall she found a pleasant and available bellboy, on his way to the floor of the house. He chatted with her until they reached the closed doors guarded by a doorman. The bellboy went merrily on his way.

"It always seems to me that they know more, younger, than I ever knew," the doorman commented.

"He has a good line," Abby agreed. "I need to go in."

"The house is in recess." Very suddenly the agreeable older man had become the guardian of empire. He held one protective hand on the handle of the door.

"I don't mind," Abby said, doing her best to look just a little more naive than she was. "I have a message for my husband."

"I'd be glad to deliver it for you, lady."

"It's—not quite that kind of message." A little stammer made it all sound so reasonable. "He left early—and we had a fight, and——"

"Ah. I understand." The doorman, who looked to be Irish and was most probably Anglo-Spanish, nodded his head sagely. The doors behind him swung open, and a congressman scurried out. "And what might the name of this husband of yours be?"

"Farnsworth," she said. "A big, tall, husky——"

The doorman held up one hand as a stop sign. "No need to describe him," he said, chuckling. "The congressman from Ohio. He's been all day up and down about the agriculture bill, setting fires to a lot of dis-

tinguished tails in the house, insulting his elders, and
using language that bordered close on getting him thrown
out. Oh, yes, indeed, I know the congressman from Ohio.
And I think he's the only member left in the chamber.
Just let me have a peek.''

He was back in a moment. "Only one," he con-
firmed. "But the House will be in session in—oh, fifteen
minutes, so you'd better hurry."

"Why is that?" Abby asked. "Are they afraid of mind
pollution?''

"Don't quote me," the doorman said, "but you can't
pollute what you haven't got. Get you in, lass." It required two hands to swing one of the bronze doors wide.
Abby squeezed through into the echoing, almost empty
chamber. The door closed behind her with a sort of hiss.

"Get you in, lass." Irish, or a Scot? She scanned the
semicircle of seats in front of her. Up on the podium a
young secretary was dividing some documents into separate piles. And to her left, all the way up at the top of
the chamber, in what had to be the least desirable seat
of all the four hundred and thirty-five, Congressman
Selby Farnsworth, with his shoulders hunched over, his
eyes half closed, was occasionally banging a fist lightly
on the desk in front of him.

"Selby?" Even though the room was empty she whispered, awed by the fact that government lived and
reigned under this roof. Farnsworth stirred not a muscle.
Climb up, Abby demanded. Her feet responded carefully, treating the carpeted floor as if it were a Persian
rug. And maybe it is, she told herself as she stopped to
scan the floor. Newspapers were always blaming Congress for wild indiscretions—but this was an ordinary
rug. With a stain on one of the risers, for that matter.

The higher she went, the more nervous she became. "Selby?" She was almost at his elbow by this time.

"I told you people I didn't want to be disturbed," he grumbled, and only then did he look up. "Abby. My Lord, Abby, what are you doing here?"

"Looking for you," she said. He came slowly to his feet, shrugging his suit jacket down, and replacing his pen in the little well cut for it in the desk top.

"It's still warfare?" he asked.

"I want——"

"Where the hell did you disappear to?" he interrupted. "Everybody stopped to celebrate, and you were gone!"

"You could have asked around," she said. "Did you?"

"Did I? Hell, no. Why should I ask around when my darling bride just ups and walks out on me? I'd like to wring your neck." Instead he grabbed her, lifted her off her feet, and very thoroughly kissed her. There was a moment or two of applause, as more pages and a couple of adults had joined the small group down by the podium.

"As it happened," she raged at him, "I didn't think I was getting married at all. I thought it was just a dumb show. Did you know better, Farnsworth?"

"Know better what?" he grumbled. He's looking more like a bear every minute, she told herself as she backed off one stair. But I'm not going to give up! I'm not!

"I got this letter in the mail this morning," she said, waving the envelope in his face.

"I congratulate you," he said stiffly. "Some day we'll get the post office to deliver *all* the mail all the time!"

"Don't be so—darned imperial," she snarled at him. "If you people in Congress worked as hard as mail

carriers do the nation would be on top of the world."
She stopped to shove her mass of hair out of her face.
"It's this *particular* letter. Look at the return address."

He used one hand to steady her own, as he read.
"Church of the——" he read. "Reverend Mr. Playfair.
Where have I heard that name before?"

"Stop stalling," she yelled at him. "You know where.
Like just before you signed this wedding certificate."
She rattled the second paper under his nose, and almost
swore that he paled.

Down at the podium the Speaker pro tem picked up
the gavel, and then put it back down again. "Getting
late," his companion told him.

"I can't interrupt," the Speaker commented. "Look
at that girl up there with Farnsworth. Her finger's going
sixty miles an hour right under his nose. It looks as if
she's skinning him alive. I couldn't possibly give him as
effective a reprimand!" And as the several House
members wandered in it looked as if they all agreed.

"Married," she screamed at him. "That's what this
paper says. Not perhaps, not maybe. Married. Who in
God's green world would want to be married to a man
like you?"

"Hey, don't knock it till you've tried it," Selby responded. He turned off her finger pointer by seizing her
wrist and freezing it in position. "So we're married. Who
arranged for the preacher? Do you remember?"

She remembered. Great-Aunt Letty, that was who. But
Abby was certainly not going to admit it. Instead she
nibbled at her lower lip and prayed that God would strike
the Capitol building with lightning, or that the invading
British army might fire a rocket barrage, as it did in
1812, and burn the whole place down.

"So now you admit it?" He pulled her back up to the stair on which he was standing. "Your meddling, interfering aunt——"

"Great-Aunt," she interrupted.

"Great-Aunt, then. You deny that she's responsible for this terrible state of affairs?"

"I admit nothing," she said firmly. "The question is, what are we going to do about it?"

"You expect *me* to do something about it?"

"Of course I do. You're the man here. Men are supposed to take charge of things!"

"Lord be praised," he muttered. "You've finally come to your senses." He leaned over and swept her up in his arms again.

"Wha—what?"

"Shadup. I'm going to kiss you."

"I don't mind that. I mean——"

He blocked off her lips with his own. It lasted about thirty seconds, and brought applause from the audience, which at last caught their attention. "Look what you've done now," he muttered.

"You were doing all the kissing," she returned as she ducked her head into his chest. "I meant, what are we going to do about this marriage?"

"Nothing at all," he snapped. "We're married, and that's all there is to it."

"But—but——" she stuttered. "What if——?"

"What if what?"

"What if Harry doesn't approve?"

"For some crazy reason my son thinks that you're God's gift to the world, put on this earth just for him. Try again."

"My mother?"

"Your mother will be excruciatingly pleased about it. I called her up and asked her a couple of days ago! Somebody else?"

"Nobody else," she muttered, burrowing more deeply into his chest. She didn't dare ask what Great-Aunt Letty thought about it. He might gladly strangle them all. Perhaps she was being too humble?

"I have," she said firmly, "several very large brothers, who——"

"Who can't understand why you haven't married before. Any other arguments?"

"I—guess not," she said, sighing. "Only it seems so—uncouth, getting married like that and all. A girl has her dreams."

He tightened his grip, and turned to carry her down the stairs, when the massive gavel fell. "Young man," the Speaker said, "would you kindly kiss the girl and get her out of here so we can go about the nation's business?"

Abby tried to sit up in his arms, wrath flashing in her eyes. Selby translated. "My wife feels that this whole affair is very uncouth, Mr. Speaker, and intends to have a great deal to say—for the rest of my life, she tells me, unless something is done——"

"I'm not here to——" The Speaker pro tem felt a tug on his arm. He leaned over, and had his ear bent by the elected Speaker, a man of no mean power. The new man gaveled a time or two, cleared his throat, and pounded the gavel one more time.

"It is the sense of this House," he announced, "considering the large number of women who are not only registered, but who actually vote, to recognize this—joining, and to grant to the congressman from Ohio and his wife the freedom of the house—but not just at this time. All in favor?" And before a single member could say Rumpelstiltskin the hammer fell again. "The ayes have it," the Speaker announced. "Now, will you kindly kiss the lady and get her out of here?"

"I don't see why not," Selby Farnsworth said as he bent to the work. They were still indulging when Selby carried her out of the chamber, and back to the shadows of the east portico. He put her down.

"I've got to go into training," he grumbled, "or you've got to go on a diet."

"Indeed you should," she said primly. "Exercise, I mean. I understand that full-time marriage can be a very physical thing. Oh, by the way, I met your first wife over at your house."

"Good God."

"Don't use the Lord's name in vain."

"Lecture me tomorrow. What did she want?"

"Money. Well, she asked to take Harry away, but would have preferred money."

"You stopped her? Harry's still at home?"

"I stopped her. I made her an offer she couldn't refuse. Harry's at home—at your home——"

"At our home," he interjected.

"Yes, at our home, and Cleo is there guarding him. Only now I don't know——" How they were going to get home, she meant to say, but he cut her off with a quick kiss.

"I'll survive," he said somewhat boastfully. "I have plenty of stamina. I don't know about you."

"My stamina is not in question here," she said as her eyes followed a movement across the square. She snatched a quick kiss. "But I'm glad you've got plenty of muscle power." Over his shoulder she could see the district's tow truck wheel up and connect itself to his congressional car. "Can we walk all the way back to the house?"

"Walk back? What an idiotic idea. I'm saving all my strength for tonight. We're just going to hunt up the place where you parked and——" The congressman from Ohio took a deep breath as he watched the little procession go up the street in front of them. "My car?"

"Community property," she said. "Everything we own we share together. And yes, that's our car the police are towing away!"

"Maybe I made a mistake," he mused. "I can't afford a cab."

"Oh, and I forgot to tell you. Your former wife has remarried. That's why she claimed she needed the money."

Selby whooped like an Indian chasing Custer's soldiers at the Little Big Horn. "Married! Hot damn! That means the alimony stops on her wedding day. Maybe I can afford a cab. Maybe I can afford *you*! Or hire a lawyer about this wedding business."

"Too late now," she said, laughing. "I've got it in writing. You might as well give up the struggle and kiss me again."

Which he did.

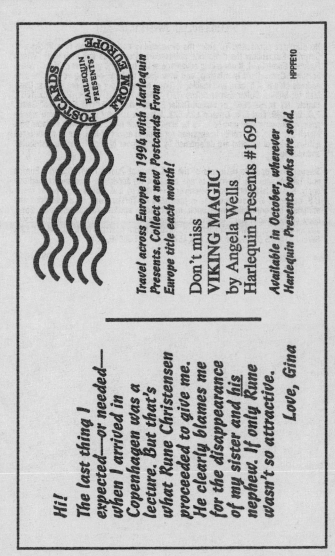

POSTCARDS FROM EUROPE

HARLEQUIN PRESENTS®

Hi!

The last thing I expected—or needed— when I arrived in Copenhagen was a lecture. But that's what Rune Christensen proceeded to give me. He clearly blames me for the disappearance of my sister and his nephew. If only Rune wasn't so attractive.

Love, Gina

Travel across Europe in 1994 with Harlequin Presents. Collect a new Postcards From Europe title each month!

Don't miss
VIKING MAGIC
by Angela Wells
Harlequin Presents #1691

Available in October, wherever
Harlequin Presents books are sold.

HPPFE10

MILLION DOLLAR SWEEPSTAKES (III)

HARLEQUIN®

THE VENGEFUL GROOM
Sara Wood

Legend has it that those married in Eternity's chapel are destined for a lifetime of happiness. But happiness isn't what Giovanni wants from marriage—it's revenge!

Ten years ago, Tina's testimony sent Gio to prison—for a crime he didn't commit. *Now* he's back in Eternity and looking for a bride. *Now* Tina is about to learn just how ruthless and disturbingly sensual Gio's brand of vengeance can be.

THE VENGEFUL GROOM, available in October from Harlequin Presents, is the fifth book in Harlequin's new cross-line series, **WEDDINGS, INC.** Be sure to look for the sixth book, **EDGE OF ETERNITY,** by Jasmine Cresswell (Harlequin Intrigue #298), coming in November.

HARLEQUIN®
PRESENTS Plus

One brief encounter had disastrously altered their futures, leaving Antonia with deep psychological scars and Patrick accused of a horrific crime. Will the passion that exists between them be enough to heal their wounds?

Fler knows she's in for some serious heartache when she falls for Kyle Ranburn, the man who caused her daughter so much pain. But she has no idea how difficult it is to be torn by her love for the two of them.

Fall in love with Patrick and Kyle—Antonia and Fler do!

Watch for

Wounds of Passion by Charlotte Lamb
Harlequin Presents Plus #1687

and

Dark Mirror by Daphne Clair
Harlequin Presents Plus #1688

Harlequin Presents Plus
The best has just gotten better!

Available in October wherever Harlequin books are sold.

This September, discover the fun of falling in love with...

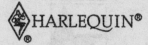

love and laughter

Harlequin is pleased to bring you this exciting new collection of three original short stories by bestselling authors!

**ELISE TITLE
BARBARA BRETTON
LASS SMALL**

LOVE AND LAUGHTER—sexy, romantic, fun stories guaranteed to tickle your funny bone and fuel your fantasies!

Available in September wherever Harlequin books are sold.